200 West Victoria Street,
, CA 93101
Knoll, Publishers
Published in 1998
ed States of America

Edition

98   5 4 3 2 1

characters and events portrayed in
esemblance to real people or events is

Cataloging-in-Publication Data

Gil Yates private investigator novel /

alk. paper)

8

98-13798
CIP

xt typeface is ITC Galliard, 11 point
n 60-pound Lakewood white, acid free paper
Case bound with Kivar 9, Smyth Sewn

DISCARDED BY THE
URBANA FREE LIBRARY

3 1230 00460 9000

URBANA FREE LIBRARY.
(217-367-4057)

S0-BAA-453
THE URBANA FREE LI

DEC 2 0 1998   DATE DUE
JUL 3 1 1998   JAN 2 0 1999
AUG 2 0 1998
                           DEC 2 0 2004
SEP 0 5 1998   JAN 0 2 2005
SEP 1 4 1998
OCT 0 4 1998   JAN 2 4 2007
NOV 0 4 1998   MAR 1 9 2008
NOV 2 1 1998   FEB 2 1 2012
DEC 1 1 1998

Allen A. Knoll, Publishers,
Santa Barbara
© 1998 by Allen A
All rights reserved.
Printed in the Unit

First

05 04 03 02 01 00 99

This is a work of fiction. The
this book are fictitious, and n
coincidental.

Library of Congress

Boyle, Alistair.
    Bluebeard's last stand : a
by Alistair Boyle. --1st ed
    p.   cm.
    ISBN 1-888310-45-6 (
    I. Title.
PS3552.0917B58   199
813'.54--dc21

ALLEN

Printed

Also by Alistair Boyle

The Unlucky Seven
The Con
The Missing Link

It was raining the day I met Harvey Cavendish, and rain fit him to a T. He was so gloomy. I'd never seen a young man so gloomy. You might have guessed he wanted to talk to me about his mother.

It didn't rain that often in these parts of Southern California, and navigating the narrow, winding streets of Palos Verdes in this soup was horrendous.

It gave me a weird foreboding about undertaking the task Harvey Cavendish had called about. If you can imagine people still being named Cavendish. I looked it up in the hope of getting some insight into Harvey's character. Cavendish means tobacco softened, sweetened, and pressed into cakes.

On the phone Harvey had both apology and pleading in his voice. Soft tobacco all right. Yet he seemed to be on guard about being taken advantage of. And then there was the undercurrent of paranoia.

From what he told me on the phone, I had the sinking suspicion that I was to be employed on behalf of greed— never a pleasant prospect unless I could get in on the action.

Harvey said a man was going to kill his mother for her fortune. He wanted me to prevent it. If I were interested, he said it would be worth my while to talk to him.

That was it in the nuts, he said. Or something like that. Clichés are not my forte. Much as I love them, I usually garble them, but I get the sense of them if I do say so myself. That's the nut's shell of it.

Harvey told me I was recommended by the Swiss counsel where his wife worked. She had made inquiries of her superiors who in turn inquired of the Swiss police which led to Jane Eaton at Interpol, God bless her. She had gotten me my most celebrated case—my last one—where this nut was systematically bombing *The Unlucky Seven* whom he thought were ruling the world.

On the surface this seemed smaller French fries, but almost as bizarre.

I don't know how I got through that foggy rain on those winding roads to Harvey's house, but apparently I had.

Harvey and Meridith Cavendish's housing tract in Rancho Palos Verdes had been carved out of the hillside by a real estate developer not long on aesthetic sense. He sent his bulldozer corps across the hill laterally, at four different levels, to carve out four straight streets, setting his houses only on the view side like those little plastic houses along the edge of a Monopoly board. He then gave the streets French names for a touch of class.

Class always appealed to Harvey Cavendish.

The houses on Harvey's street all had five-digit addresses and all looked alike. If you started at 1st Street in downtown Los Angeles, Harvey lived on 300th Street.

Old Tobacco, as I had come to fondly think of him, opened the front door of his house and said, "Oh, Mr. Yates," as though he had forgotten I was coming. "Ah, come in," he added, as though he weren't sure that was a good idea.

Abstract was my word for him. Distracted, maybe.

Harvey Cavendish was a tall guy with a gut who looked like he had put black shoe polish on his hair. The poor man was going bald and was utilizing all the desperation tactics of emergent baldness, *viz.* letting the remaining hair grow extra-long and combing it over the bald spot. When he moved, it seemed to take inner strength and resolve. I'll bet Harvey always looked tired.

2

The inside of the house was tastefully, if not elegantly, furnished. Swiss modern, sort of, with a lived-in feeling. The big picture windows faced the ocean, the drapes were open, but all I could see was gray gloom.

"Nice house," I said, looking around Harvey's place on the hill overlooking the ocean.

"Just a tract," he said. "Nothing like I could have if you do your job. I have aspirations," he said, leaving me no doubt his were in the plutocratic direction. "Well, you don't look like much," he said phrenologizing me and scrutinizing my physique. "Not the kind of guy anyone is liable to mistake for a detective or some macho stud."

"Thank you," I said, bowing with my eyes. It takes one to know one, I thought.

Then *she* came into the room, and everything else went comatose. Sometime, somewhere in the haze Old Tobacco said, "This is my wife, Meridith."

I think I nodded and smiled, but I couldn't be sure.

She was statuesque and lithe with bright flaxen hair and perfect teeth, and had a body that could have closed down a seminary.

Meridith poured herself into the couch at the far end, like steaming coffee going from pot to cup.

There was no hiding my admiration for Harvey's distaff, nor was there any hiding of Harvey's disdain for it.

To bridge this embarrassing gap, Harvey thrust a stack of photocopied papers into my hands. "Newspaper clippings," he said. "Some easier to read than others."

A cursory glance at them gave me a quick insight into the man now answering to Reginald Windsor, who began life as Fred Kantor, and in-between had operated under various other aliases.

Our Reginald, it seems, had been quite a Bluebeard in his time. I speak, of course, of *the* Bluebeard—the folklore character who made a name for himself by marrying and murdering a series of hapless, hopeless and helpless women. And the fear, of course, was that Reginald was still at it.

He'd had about nine wives, albeit a number of them overlapping, and a distressing number of them having met with untimely accidental deaths.

Reginald had now set his cap for Harriet Himmelfarb, understandably distressing her son by her first marriage, Harvey Cavendish.

"The thing I don't understand," gloomy Harvey said in his dark, high-low voice, "is that Reginald, or whatever you want to call him, is an accomplished tennis coach, and they make oodles of money."

"Not enough for him, apparently," I said.

"Apparently," he agreed reluctantly. "It says in that Pinkerton report I had done, it is the game that challenges him. We used to call them conquests. See how many women you could get."

I wondered how many women Harvey had gotten, but I didn't ask. Malvin Stark (my moniker in the real world) was not too accomplished at those shenanigans—as my marriage to the ample Tyranny Rex will amply testify. As Private Detective Gil Yates, I am a different kettle of gefilte fish.

The dining room opened to the living room and shared its spectacular view of the Pacific. Harvey sat at the dining room table and motioned for me to join him. I cast a last glance of disappointment at Meridith seated across the room on the couch and sat as bidden. And as bidden was with my back to Meridith; it was not a happy state of affairs.

Harvey seemed to want me to read the clippings, so I did, carefully taking my time. It wasn't a pretty story. One of Reginald's four victims had drowned in the bathtub, another went out the window of a tall building in New York, another fell down the stairs of their home, a fourth was hit by a train while she was unconscious in a car from which Reginald had escaped. He said the car had stalled and he didn't have time to save his wife.

There had been no prosecutions, though the railroad case did result in an indictment.

When I finished reading the photocopies, I looked up at Harvey.

"I don't have to tell you who his next victim will be if we don't do something about it."

"Have you talked to your mother about this?" I waved at the clippings.

"She's just like a child," Harvey said. "If you forbid her something, she wants it all the more. And I can't stop her. I don't know anybody who can."

"But what does she say?"

"Oh, that he's older now, more mature. And she loves him. She never had a man treat her so well. Of course I argue, but she doesn't hear me. I say 'What if he kills you?' and she says, 'So what? I'm seventy-six—I'd die happy.'"

I threw up my hands to say—"So? It's her life"—but he stopped the thought with his own hand gesture which was sharp enough to cut a flag pole in half.

"And we'd be cut out of our money." Harvey shook his head to let me know what he thought of that.

"Certainly she can arrange it so you get it."

"Can, but won't. Stubborn. Maybe she thinks if she gives it to her kids now, Reginald will drop her like a hot potato." I liked that one. I would probably mangle it later.

"Is it in trust?"

"Yes," he said. "She can't spend the principal, but she can will it to whomever she chooses. And if she *doesn't* make a will, it goes to her kids—unless she's married."

"Then it goes to her husband?" I asked.

"Exactly!" he said.

"What does your mother say?"

"She just loves it that I'm so worried. She finds it amusing," he said, leaving no doubt he was *not* amused.

"What about the police?"

"Hah! They say come back after he kills her. They won't do anything."

"So, what do you want from me?"

"She and Reginald have decided to go on a cruise. I can keep my eye on them while they are in California—but on the high seas?" he shrugged. "Impossible. Just the place for a romantic wedding at sea with a wedding gift from groom to bride of a custom-made pair of concrete shoes."

"You think he'd *do* that?"

"Look at the clippings. He's sixty-two, she's seventy-six. What else does he want with her?"

I couldn't answer him.

"I thought we could put you on the ship—in the next penthouse. Bug it. Keep him from marrying her—and if you can't do that, at least keep her alive."

I was wondering how I might accomplish a task so elusive when he said, "I understand you work on contingency—and don't charge for expenses. What would you charge to take the case? Assuming you achieved my goals, of course."

"How long is the cruise?"

"Twenty-one days," he said. "San Francisco to Wellington, New Zealand. It stops in Los Angeles before crossing the Pacific, but they want to get on in San Francisco—same price—more glamour."

How much could I get out of this turkey for three weeks work? "How much is at stake here?" I asked.

"Her estate is worth about fifteen million and rising daily, the way the stock market is acting."

I was going to lowball the thing until I heard that. A quick calculation sent the figure $150,000 through my head. One percent of the take seemed reasonable. I asked for it in cash.

He blanched. I sensed trouble. "You can't come up with it?"

"Well, I don't know. I write her checks, but I don't know if I can get that much by her. Besides, Reginald could come up with a scheme for tying it up."

I didn't see what that could be and told him so. He didn't know either.

But I wouldn't put anything past that murderer. I was considering a couple of angles to appease him when the phone rang. Harvey leapt at it like a drowning man at a life buoy. The phone was on the wall above the counter that separated the kitchen from the dining room.

"Hello," he said. "Oh, hello, Harriet. Hold on will you, I'm going to another phone." He turned to Meridith, "Hang it up, will you?"

He set the phone down and moved quickly to a door which led to the bedrooms. The door was open, but when he got beyond it, he closed it.

Meridith was dutifully at the kitchen counter with the phone at her ear. I heard Harvey yell through the closed door: "Hang it up, Meridith," as though she had a notion to disobey him. She replaced the receiver.

"That's his mother," Meridith said redundantly. "He'll be on the phone for hours."

"He's very attached to her?"

She smiled. "You might say that. You might also say he sucks up to her for financial reasons."

I always like to talk to the women. Less baloney.

Without seeming to sound like I was astonished at the disparate match, I asked how she happened to marry Harvey.

She smiled a broad, dazzling, but bemused smile.

"I wanted a successful businessman," she said, "and instead I got a poet who doesn't write poetry. Harvey is a Bohemian with aspirations to royalty. He was born to be an aristocrat because he has no inkling to work."

"Why did you marry him?"

She shrugged her pretty shoulders. "Biological clock, citizenship. The usual mercenary justifications for the usual less-than-ideal marriage. I was almost thirty, languishing in Zurich with sporadic dates with assorted wimps and perverts. My father was a civil servant, much given to order. I inherited his love of security. I wanted a man who could make me secure. There was money in Harvey's family." She shrugged, "I'm not ashamed of that; I'm just disappointed it's been harder to get at than I expected." She sighed, "But I'm a patient woman. The way Harriet treats herself, we shouldn't have long to wait."

"How's that?"

"Drinks. Nonstop. It fits right into Bluebeard's

modus operandi. Oh dear," she said, turning on the flashing eyelashes, "I must sound terribly selfish."

"You mean you're not?" I asked playfully.

She laughed. "No, I am. I just wish I had more talent for hiding it. We've been living off my father and mother. They bought this house for us. I have to go into Los Angeles to work every day. Takes me an hour at rush hour."

"Does Harvey work?"

"Not so you could notice. He's had a series of jobs, but they don't last."

"Why not?"

She wrinkled her nose. "Personality mostly, I guess. He can be difficult."

"What way?"

"I don't know. A spoiled child way, I guess. He's in business for himself now—accounting—doesn't have many clients though. Stays home most of the time. Cooks, keeps house, waits for his inheritance. Then when he gets it, I can quit my politics-riddled job at the embassy. Give up my killing commute."

"Why don't you live closer to town?"

"Where? Watts? Someplace where the property costs zillions of dollars? We found this tract next to prestigious Palos Verdes Estates, close enough for Harvey to rationalize listing his address as Palos Verdes Estates. He was *born* to be upper class."

"But he's a trained accountant?"

"Yes."

"He likes numbers?" I asked.

She smiled. "If they have a dollar sign before them." She had the cutest accent. A soft, lilting German. "My father was frugal. He devoted his life to storing up Swiss francs for his darling only child. He wanted to make my life easier. He hadn't reckoned with my marrying Harvey Cavendish. So, as I say, now Harvey's interest in and aptitude for numbers is limited to preserving his mother's estate for himself and for converting his father-in-law's hard-earned Swiss francs into good old-fashioned American dollars."

I should have a father-in-law like that.

Just then Harvey returned to the room looking like death was his best friend.

"They're talking marriage," he said, like an undertaker who had buried his girlfriend. "She thinks it would be cute to do it on the ship."

2

Harvey Cavendish looked like a soft tobacco cake standing in his doorway bidding me goodbye. I tried to steal a last look at Meridith while I heard Harvey say, "I'll get a contract drawn. I'll bring it over. What's your address?"

I held up my hand to staunch the bloody thought. "I'm private," I said. "Enhances my confidentiality."

"Well," he sputtered, "I can't do business with a man who won't give me his address."

I shrugged. "Suit yourself," I said.

"But, what if I want to see you?"

"You have my phone number."

"But...but you don't answer there."

"I'll call you back—I did before."

He shook his head. It was clearly unacceptable to him.

I turned a palm up to indicate I could not care less. We were getting accomplished at body language.

I walked away from the house down the short path to my car. I heard more sputtering from Old Tobacco Cakes, but if he was saying anything intelligible, I couldn't understand it.

I had driven my car to the entrance sign of Harvey's subdivision on Palos Verdes Drive West before I sensed the car behind me. A check in my rearview mirror confirmed my worst—it was Harvey Soft Tobacco. The sucker was following me.

I slammed on the parking brake, and leapt out of the car to confront him. He rolled down his window—

"What are you doing?" I snarled.

"Following you."

I shook my head. "Sorry, No can do."

"I didn't want you going away mad. Do we have a deal?" There was a catch in his voice.

"Not if you want to play snoop."

"I promise…" he said. There were tears in his eyes. "I'll call you when I've drawn the contract." he said, his voice quaking.

I got in my car and pulled away. In my rearview mirror, I could see Harvey making a U-turn.

At home, my Tyranny Rex was schlepping rigid cardboard boxes of her glass figurines preparatory to another sale featuring her loss leaders. Everything she sold turned into a loss leader that led nowhere. I always said, if anyone ever expressed the slightest interest in her glass junk, Tyranny would kiss him and pay him to take it. Some saleswoman. Her goal was to get as many of those urinating farm boys and defecating cows into circulation as possible, thereby creating a widespread appreciation and burgeoning demand for her work. Sort of like writing.

This was my partner in irreconcilable differences, Dorcas, whom I lovingly nicknamed Tyranny Rex for the dinosaur of a strikingly similar name. This was not only because she seemed to me to be as large as a dinosaur (she wasn't—quite) or because she had the appetites of a dinosaur, but rather because when you were in the presence of a dinosaur there wasn't any question who was boss.

Tyranny and I had raised (in a manner of speaking) two children. August was named for his grandfather, Elbert August Wemple, by Tyranny Rex, my veto being steam rollered by baby August's mother and his namesake (it only takes two-thirds and that's what they had). Though I suppose if you had to pick one of those three names, August is surely the least of the evils. And August has become a ballet dancer, a fact that drives his namesake insane. I never was one for forcing kids in or out of professions, but I'm kind of tickled at what August's vocation has done to his grandfather, Daddybucks. He refuses to talk about him and that's one less topic I have to listen to.

Our daughter, Felicity, we hear from when the well runs dry in her never-ending quest for higher education. I'm not exactly sure about how high her education might be, but I *do* know it certainly is long.

"Oh, there you are," Tyranny Rex said, when she saw me in her path. She always greeted me like I had been the object of a long and arduous search. "You can give me a hand with these boxes," she said, as though I had been chafing at the bit to do so. Ordinarily I eschewed helping with the grunt work. It was my one holdout against the power of the Wemples. But now I thought it might be polite.

The remarkable thing about Tyranny's glass figurine operation was how often she seemed to return from a sale with more boxes than she *took* to the sale. I used to ask her about this, but the best she ever came up with was that she packed more carefully before a show so it required fewer boxes.

The inside of the house became more cluttered with the figurines every day. Tyranny was not shackled by any of the ordinary, supply-and-demand constraints. And since she could make the little darlings faster than she could sell them, she just did. Daddybucks was underwriting the insanity anyway. Fine, I thought, let him store them. But that was not an idea whose time had flourished.

Tyranny Rex had a bevy of ballerinas. She seemed to delight in turning out one after the other of them. One day I asked her why there were no male ballet dancers to compliment the ballerinas. I knew what the answer was going to be, but when you are in my painfully subordinate position, you have to stick in the pins when you can.

"I don't think it would be very nice to remind Daddy Wemple of August's chosen profession. It makes him so mad just to *think* about it."

So she made the urinating little boy instead. I honestly don't think either Tyranny or Daddybucks saw the great irony of it. This was what August was doing to Daddybucks and his vast wealth, but both Tyranny and her even more tyrannical father thought the urinating lad the cutest piece they ever saw.

While we were carrying in the boxes to clutter the house even more—we dropped them willy-billy wherever we found a vacant space on the floor—I started talking to Tyranny from behind her. In a way talking to her back was more pleasant than talking to her front.

"Dorcas," I muttered. I didn't dare call her Tyranny Rex to her face, or even to her back for that matter. "Ah, I have, ah, the opportunity to, ah, go to New Zealand with the Palm Society for its international meeting.... It's going to be about three weeks in November...on a ship." I was such a lousy liar.

"There," she said, "Over there," she pointed to a bare spot on the dining-room table for me to deposit my box of glass figurines. I realized I had asked her at the perfect time—when she was preoccupied with her own affairs, proving, once again when you wanted something you could do a lot worse than talking to your wife's back.

But suddenly she whirled around, "What did you say?"

"I'm, ah, thinking of going to the meeting of the International Palm Society in November." Then I added my big bluff— "Want to come along?"

"How long is it?"

"About three weeks."

"Three weeks! I never heard of such a thing. They have jet airplanes now, you know."

"It's going to be on a ship. I mean I'd go on a ship. We stop in Tahiti where they have a great palm collection in their botanic garden. Why don't you go along?" I stepped up the brazenness of my question.

"A ship? No way. Daddy Wemple took me on a ship when I was in high school. I've never been so bored in my life. Never again."

"That's too bad," I said. "I thought it might be fun."

"Besides I'm booked all through November. It's completely out of the question."

Of course if she had thrown her arms around me and said, "Whooeeee, I'd love to go," I would have had to waltz to different music.

I realized later as I prepared to sign the agreement with Harvey Cavendish that there was something missing from the canned marriage vows. They didn't say anything about telling the truth.

So what was for so many years a disadvantage turned to my advantage. The king and princess of self-absorption who were a pain in the posterior in the early years have turned into a convenience now that I'm in the contingency investigating racket. Imagine bringing off a three-week cruise with a normal wife and employer. And with such audacity. A palm meeting in New Zealand! There are hardly *any* palm trees in New Zealand. But Daddybucks doesn't know palm trees from a Three Day Notice to Pay or Quit, and Tyranny Rex cares only for glass figurines. I realize now I could have told them I was going to Antarctica to study tropical palms and I'd have gotten the same reaction. Daddybucks thinks I have a girlfriend. So, I told some more lies, and watched old dandruff head leer in vicarious pleasure at the thought of little me making it big with the femmes.

"Go, go!" he said, waving at me from his elevated platform in the warehouse of Elbert A. Wemple Realty. "You're taking more vacations than Carter has liver pills, so don't expect to be paid for your time. God knows it's only my unabashed generosity that allows me to pay you while you *are* here."

He was all gall bladder, that one.

3

I had a telephone message from Harvey Cavendish. The contract was ready. I drove up to Palos Verdes to get it.

It was unacceptable. Why is it these unemployed rich guys always seem so bent on grinding the poor?

We met in his glass-walled living room. Meridith, his gorgeous wife, was out working, Harvey was not. The sun was streaming in the west windows and I realized you could fry in this environment. Harvey did not close the drapes because then his living room would be just another tract house without the view. I read the one-page offering on the spot.

"Hey," I said, "I'm not crazy. I could never sign this."

"Why not?" They always sounded surprised—like they really didn't know what you had agreed on.

"First of all, I'm not paying for the cruise you want me to go on."

"But you came recommended because you don't nickel and dime for expenses."

"Forty grand is not nickel and dime."

"This is an expense," he said. "I just thought..."

"You thought wrong," I said.

"Okay," he said, "I'll change it to read we'll pay it if you succeed with the rest of it. Keep her alive, get rid of him or get him to sign a prenuptial agreement."

"Get rid of him? You want me to kill him?"

"I wouldn't mind," he said, "but that's not what I meant. Get him out of the picture. Get him lined up with a younger woman. There are always single women on those cruises."

Wow, and he wanted me to play matchmaker. What a guy. He should work for my father-in-law.

"So, will that change be acceptable?" he asked.

I stared at him a moment to try to divine if he really thought I would buy that. I simply shook my head and stood up. "I'll tell you what," I said. "I'm no longer interested in working for you. But if you find someone willing to pay forty-thousand dollars for a penthouse for the pleasure of breaking up your seventy-six-year-old mother's romance, I'll pay you a thousand dollars just to meet him."

He changed the agreement. I felt a little sorry for him. He was trying to be macho and have some sway over me, but I'd had enough of that at home to last me a lifetime. And seeing him last night with his breadwinner beauty, I figured he must have a similar situation. I was overcoming mine with this private eye schtick. Let Harvey find his own salvation.

To add to my cover, I took scores of pictures of my palms and cycads as if I were going to take them along for show-and-tell time at the International Palm Conference. I flaunted the pictures at home for Tyranny, but she had no interest in plants. Glass was her bag. Glass was fragile like Tyranny was not. I often wondered what a creative psycho-analyst could do with that.

I would take the pictures along on the cruise, like taking a picture of a girlfriend so you won't forget what she looks like.

Before I left on this eventful trip, I had to contract with someone to look after my palms and cycads. I knew I couldn't count on Tyranny, she was booked. So I got a young girl a few doors down on the street. She seemed to take an interest in growing things.

My passport was still good, so it was just a matter of packing the right things. November would be cool on both ends of the cruise and hot in the middle.

Then there was the electronic surveillance equipment. I made a few calls, starting with a guy at the phone company and played real dumb. He gave me some names. I went to see one of them and walked away with some good stuff for just under eight hundred dollars.

I had a final meeting with Harvey and was broken-hearted his wife Meridith was, once again, not in residence. It was in his glassy living room. The drapes still stood open, and I had a stronger sense that Harvey defined himself by his view of the ocean. But it was foggy again and we couldn't see any water at all.

"When I get this money that's rightfully mine," he said, "I'm moving up to Rolling Hills—behind the gates—the weather is a lot better. More sun. This fog is depressing."

"Well, you could move down to Torrance with us flatlanders," I said. "Not much fog there."

"No, thanks," he said, leaving no room for speculation about what he thought of that modest idea. "Now, Mr. Yates," he continued in a grave manner, "I can't impress on you enough how *critical* your mission is. I know you could lose a hundred and fifty thousand if you fail, but I could lose millions."

Harvey didn't mince, and I hope he didn't see me wince.

"I'll do my best," I said.

"And I hope it's good enough." I noticed a subtle change in his attitude toward me now that I was an employee of his. "I'm absolutely convinced this so-called Reginald person is bound and determined to get my mother to sign everything over to him and then kill her for it. I think it's all going to happen on this cruise—and you are my only hope to prevent it."

I asked if I could have a copy of the Pinkerton Security and Investigation Services background report on Reginald Windsor a.k.a. Fred Kantor, and Harvey disappeared into the nether regions of the house and produced it. I scanned it enough to verify that Harvey had given me a pretty accurate picture of Reginald's past, and it wasn't pretty.

"Have you considered a restraining order?"

He shook his head. "She'd end up hating me so much she'd disinherit me," he said. "It's all so unfair. We're entitled to that money by birth. Grandfather knew that. Yet he put in that stupid clause. I mean it's like he didn't trust her enough to just *give* her the money outright, he put it in a trust fund instead so she couldn't get at it. But apparently he trusted her enough to let her will it to whomever she wanted—which just acts as another club she has over my sister and me. I'm tired of being subjugated by my mother. This money will finally give me the independence I deserve."

He sure thought he deserved a lot, and that grew out of a mysterious birthright. What would he do with seven and a half million?

"Do you have any children?" I asked.

"Not yet. Meridith is still young. There's time—if we had assurance of financial security."

I wondered if he wanted the money as a hold on his pretty blond wife. Inheritance is sole and separate property, so she couldn't cry divorce and get half. An interesting thought. I kept it to myself.

The way I doped it out, Harriet wasn't getting any younger and that gave Harvey hope. He was not a guy given to maudlin sentiment about his dear mother: wanting to save her life for her sake or for the wonderful contributions she could still make to mankind, I suppose by spending her money. No, Harvey called a spade a shovel, and he was willing to dig his mother's final resting place if he could be assured of his "rightful" inheritance. All I had to do, really, was to oversee a foolproof prenuptial agreement, and in the absence of that, all I had to do was keep her alive.

It didn't even *sound* simple.

4

I am living the life of a sybarite. But don't run for your dictionary, I'm going to tell you what it means.

I didn't know what it meant until I got the cruise catalogue which beckoned me to

live the life of a sybarite
("anyone very fond of luxury and pleasure: voluptuary").

That's me, a voluptuary
("a person devoted to luxurious living and sensual pleasures").

I have signed on the ship as Gil Yates, not my *nom de plume*, but the name I have accidentally attached to my private investigating biz. I say "accidentally" because I more or less backed into this line of work as an escape from the ordinarily mundane life I lead as a property manager in the employ of my frugal father-in-law, Old Dandruff Head, who heretofore has only controlled those portions of my life that my wife did not.

As a result of a series of bizarre happenstances, I was to be a passenger on this luxurious ship, installed not in a mere cabin, but in a PENTHOUSE, by the very people who hired me to look after their mother.

And not only was I in the penthouse next door to

19

the loving couple, but I was seated at their table in the dining room. And they didn't know that they were being monitored, so to speak. They thought I was some ordinary Joe who just happened to have enough dough to afford a penthouse on a twenty-one-day cruise from San Francisco to Wellington, New Zealand.

To tell the truth, I considered blowing some of the windfall from my first case on an ocean voyage, but then the voice of reason blasted in my ear and I thought better of it. And a good thing too, because my second case was as much a financial bust as the first case was a smasheroo success. My third case put me in the black again, thanks to my saving the skin of Harold Mattlock, one of the richest men in the world.

I was careful to keep out of the line of sight of the happy love birds in the passageway. I didn't want them to know I was next door.

I had boarded first. It was all coordinated with Harvey so I could be on the veranda of my penthouse with my binoculars watching Reginald and Harriet climb aboard.

The Regal Nordic Sun was a fairly new ship, and it looked top-heavy as a result of the ship owners wanting to put virtually all the cabins on the outside, high up. So, on top of the hull were stacked what looked like fairly simple and ghostly white uniform apartments. The first time I laid eyes on the ship, I thought it was going to tip over.

There was a row of cabin stewards and waiters to greet the new arrivals and escort us to our cabins, where they told us our luggage would be along shortly. These stewards seemed to be a jolly lot, but I couldn't help wondering what went through their minds as all these haves clamored on board with their Ralph Lauren outfits and Mark Cross luggage and their utter self-absorption. What did they say to each other at the end of the day? Maybe they were too pooped to say anything—dragged out not from dragging the luggage that would "be along shortly," but from keeping those happy faces from cracking in the line of duty. I noticed how patiently the stewardesses were speaking to the very old passengers. It must have been like working in a geriatric clinic.

A swarthy guy with "Salvatore" on his golden label showed me to my cabin. It was a knockout. It was the size of three regular cabins and had a king-sized bed that could be closed off from the rest of the suite. There were two desks built of walnut and mahogany. The bathroom was two compartments lined with a pale yellow marble. There were two sinks, two leather couches of a deep watermelon skin hue. The bedspread matched the drapes which spanned the entire outer wall, including the sliding glass door that let you out onto a veranda that could hold twenty people, easy. There was a wing chair in a paler watermelon fabric, and all these lively colors were complimented in the drapes and bedspread, giving the place the aura of muted, happy good taste.

There were mirrors everywhere. You could stand at any point in this penthouse cabin and see yourself. The entire wall in front of one of the desks was mirror. They must have done some in-depth psychological studies that told them rich people like to look at themselves.

I went out on my veranda and saw there was a solid steel wall between the penthouses. I heard the voice of a man above me saying, "This is the life, Linda," and it was.

My cabin was on the port side. That's left (same number of letters as port) looking at the front (the bow). The stern is the back—just remember "b" comes before "s" in the alphabet—so—bow is the front. With very little more knowledge, I could have been a navy man.

Off the bow, I could see the Oakland Bay Bridge and some low, washed out olive drab dock buildings. A tug boat made its way toward the Oakland Bridge. The low hills of Yorba Buena were in the foreground, the rolling terrain of Oakland behind.

It was fun looking over the rail of my veranda down to the dock, watching all the passengers stop and paste happy smiles on their faces for the ship's photographer, who was planted between them and the gangplank. The gulls were squeaking happily. A friendly sound, I thought, that we were not liable to hear out at sea.

I perked up when Harriet and Reginald came up hand in hand and looking like teenage lovebirds. Reginald was wearing an atrocious Hawaiian shirt and pink jacket, and Harriet a fur coat. The bald top of Reginald's head glimmered in the fall sun. He was stocky and seemed no taller than Harriet. She had gray hair and a hawk's nose that pointed the way for the rest of her face.

Harvey had accompanied them to the ship, so I would have no confusion about who they were. Harvey walked like his prominent gut weighed him down. I hustled down to the entry deck they call the Pacific deck to see them come aboard.

Harvey came behind carrying a small bag for his mother. He looked at me furtively.

While Reginald, Harriet and Harvey waited for the elevator to take them up to their penthouse, I took the stairs, two at a time, so I could be out of sight when they came down the passageway on the bridge deck.

Back in my room, I opened the sliding glass door to my veranda and went out. Harvey had prearranged that he would open their door so I could get a test of them talking.

Unfortunately I couldn't hear what they were saying except for small-talk exclamations about the cabin, veranda and sights. So it was up to Harvey to stand next to the common veranda wall and say at the top of his voice, "They have champagne on the promenade deck before sailing. Want to go?" The question seemed to meet with an affirmative assent, and after I heard their door slam, I quickly cased the common interior wall for an opportunity to run my electronic surveillance wire through an opening. I found it in the telephone jack behind the substantial night stand on the port side of the bed. It was a three-drawer piece of teak with gold bands outlining the drawers.

Then I went down to join the party.

Harvey said goodbye to his mother and Reginald, and before I knew it we were underway. The band was playing and champagne was flowing. I saw Alcatraz, the place where they used to put the bad boys before it got too expensive to keep them there. No one had ever escaped successfully to shore, but an economy-hysteria gripped the prison industry and that was curtains for Alcatraz. I hung back from the lovebirds and watched them guzzle champagne. He had two glasses, she three. She shivered, hugged herself and said, "Brrr, it's cold," before he put his arm around her and they went in. After a moment I followed. When I saw them go to their room I hung back long enough so they wouldn't see me follow to my cabin.

On my veranda, I saw the Golden Gate Bridge over the bow and the Oakland Bay astern. The sun had set, the light was fading, and it was a cool, crisp twilight. I was mesmerized by the pinpoints of light receding into the total blackness.

Back in my cabin penthouse I was frustrated that the soundproofing was so good I couldn't hear what my charges were saying.

I lay the surveillance paraphernalia out on the desk and went over which belonged where. It was, I suppose, a pretty simple setup, but my mechanical aptitude was as close to klutz as you could come and still be able to tie your shoes. Finally, I convinced myself I could bring it off.

Then I heard a veranda door slide open. I stepped out on my veranda and heard Reginald's voice next door.

"Harriet, come here—look at this."

"What, darling?"

"Over here at the railing—yeah, look over there— lean over a little—"

5

I had heart failure while waiting for the splash. I was afraid to lean too far over the rail for fear they'd see me. Then rationality set in and I thought Reginald wouldn't be so foolish as to push her overboard so close to shore, when he could do it miles out to sea where the chance of discovery would be much less. I expected he was just having a dry run at it; build her confidence close to railings.

Getting rid of her wouldn't do anything for him unless she had willed her estate to him or they had gotten married without Harvey knowing about it. Both, I thought, were slim possibilities. But if either happened, I was that much further from my contingency fee.

I had left my cabin door open a crack so I could hear when the neighboring door slammed shut, indicating Harriet and Reginald were vacating the cabin for dinner. I didn't have long to wait. Reginald and Harriet hustled down to dinner at the stroke of seven-thirty. As soon as they turned the corner for the elevator, I took the passageway they had vacated.

It wasn't long before a stewardess came into the passageway in her dirndl uniform. I stood outside Harriet and Reginald's door patting my pockets. As she approached, I frowned and patted my pockets in distress. I turned to the young blond stewardess, pleasingly padded, and said "I'm terribly sorry. I seem to have locked myself out without my key."

24

"No problem, sir," she said and whipped out her master key and opened the door.

"Thank you so much." I said, then slipped into the cabin. Their penthouse was just as magnificent as mine. I quickly found the telephone jack and buried the high powered microphone behind the night stand, which had three drawers. I taped it to the back and ran the wire down through the hole in the wall that was covered with a face plate. It looked just like part of the telephone setup.

Then I snooped around to see if they had brought anything extraordinary along with them, but I didn't want to rifle their goods to leave a suspicious trail so I was circumspect, looking in drawers, the walk-in closet and the medicine chests. (There were two of them in the penthouses). I saw a lot of medication, but no guns, knives or ice picks. Then I slipped back into the hallway and returned to my cabin, where I pulled the wire through the telephone jack and attached it to the back of my bedside set of drawers. The compact, Walkman-sized recording unit I stored in the bottom drawer. That night I would test it to see that the remote hardware would carry the voices through the back of the drawers. The guy at the bug shop had assured me it would be "no problem."

If the cabin stewardess should go through my drawers, the unit would appear to her just like a Walkman and should not cause any suspicion.

I counted to ten, then made my march to the dining room where I handed the maître d' at the door the card with my table assignment on it. With a flourish worthy of grand opera, he beckoned me to follow him to the table. It was a six-seater and five of the seats were already occupied. The maître d' pulled (with a flourish, of course) the one remaining chair and I found myself seated between Harriet and a striking woman who seemed absolutely delighted to be seated next to a single man.

She couldn't wait to introduce herself. She was Sophia Romanoff she said, and I thought how serendipitous to be in the company of a Romanoff and a Windsor. She pronounced it So-*fee*-ah, as though there were a scintilla of Russian blood pumping through her veins. Sophia's face was tanned from the sun, but not rough leather like my Tyranny Rex—more a smooth glove texture. On second thought, maybe Tyranny's skin *is* like glove leather: boxing gloves—to match her disposition. Sophia had a great cascade of platinum-blond hair which fell in evenly spaced waves like the swells and valleys of the surf.

Sophia Romanoff was a looker. The only one at the table. Perhaps one of the few on the ship not old enough to be a parent of mine. She had a body that broke the mold and bedroom eyes that spelled trouble. Under ordinary circumstances, I might have made a play for her, but the circumstances were anything but ordinary.

As it turned out, I didn't have to make any play for her. She took it upon herself to jiggle those bedroom eyelashes at me.

Sophia the seductress, *par excellence*.

If pressed to guess her age, I would have said she could be a touch older than she wanted to be, but I would peg her at a tad younger than Tyranny Rex, but then I don't know anyone who doesn't seem younger than Tyranny. It might be well to remember that a guy with college-age children (I) has no cause to get uppity about age. From the way her eyes glommed onto me, it was obvious she had the heart and libido of a much younger woman.

The other couple at the table put me in mind of the lion and the mouse. The man looked like that guy who played the monster with steel teeth in those spy-action movies, only not as handsome. The woman had short but fluffy gray hair and a squeaky voice. The frames of her glasses were a leopard-skin pattern that began narrowly enough at her ears, then flared wide toward the lenses.

He was a devotee of beef, having it three times a day "Rare!" And he was starting to look like a steer himself. His voice was the opposite of his companion's: deep, gruff and loud. His name, supplied only when I asked for it, was Chester Brown. Mouse, the spouse, was called Lillith. She was as thin as a nail, and more than once I longed for a hammer.

But my focus was to be on my subjects, Reginald Windsor and Harriet Himmelfarb. Up close, Reginald's bald pate was less noticeable than the view from above. He had decent hair covering on the sides and back of his round head. Reginald was a jovial fellow with a very British name and the merest trace of a Bronx accent. He paid plenty of attention to his companion.

Harriet Himmelfarb, conversely, had a German name but a very British accent, or affectation, depending on how it struck you. It struck me as a little phony at first, but then as time went on it just seemed part of her nature. She was a short woman—in the five-one to five-two range and had a proud, ramrod posture that made me remember Napoleon Bonaparte.

Harriet was a take-charge sort of person who liked to draw the maximum attention to her person. Reginald didn't appear to mind it. He seemed like a very accommodating fellow indeed.

Our table was round and at the window, which pleased everyone. Though I never saw any of them actually look out at the ocean, it seemed to be very important to all to be seated in close proximity to the water that would surround us for the whole three weeks.

"Isn't it nice we have a window table?" Harriet asked me. She was, I was soon to discover, given to asking rhetorical questions.

As soon as I had sat down, the dynamics of what I had to look forward to leaped in view.

"Well, Mr. Yates," Sophia Romanoff turned to face me. "Aren't you going to ask it?" she said, showing me a row of white teeth that would have inspired Chopin.

"Excuse me?"

"If I'm related," she said like a woman who was proud of a secret.

"Related?"

"To the real Romanoffs—you know, the Russian royalty."

"Oh, yes, well, are you?"

She wrinkled her nose noncommitally. "Is your wife along?" she asked, switching the subject to me. I was tempted to say, "Yes, she's under the table," but I realized that her question was just a fish for reassurance of my single status. She wanted me, of course, to say "Oh no, I'm not married," but I said instead "No, I'm sorry she couldn't make it. I think you two would have hit it off smashingly."

The menus were passed and we got down to the serious business at hand. Our waiter was short and roundish and had a sign on his maroon jacket breast pocket proclaiming him to be "Gorge." Chester across the table delighted in pronouncing it "Whore Hey!" But Horehay was nothing if not a good sport.

Chester was screwing up that slack-fleshed face that looked like it had had a serious run-in with a twelve wheeler. "I don't see any beef, " he groused. "I like beef. *Rare!*" His voice carried throughout the ship. It was so booming I had visions of the crew being unable to hear the commands on the bridge when Chester was speaking in the dining room.

"Hey, Whore Hey! Commere. I don't see any steak on here. What gives?"

"I can get you one, sir," Gorge said with an engaging, suck-up modesty. "Anything you want, we have it, I'll get it for you."

"I want a steak. Rare! And fries. And bring me a bottle of A.1. sauce. And, please," Chester boomed, "*Rare. Don't bring it to me well done. I want it rare,*" His voice was definitely *not* designed to function in low-ceilinged rooms—like this one.

My appetite was subsiding.

Then his wife ordered. Her voice squeaked like she had some terrible tightening of the vocal cords. I can't remember what she ordered. It was refreshingly normal. We forget the normal. Old Beefy I'll never forget.

Princess Romanoff ordered the salad with vinegar,

no oil. Gorge asked "And what else?"

"That's all," she said.

"What shall I have, dear?" Harriet Himmelfarb asked Reginald Windsor.

"What do you want, dear?" he asked, solicitous to a fault.

"Well I don't *know* or I wouldn't have asked."

"How about the chicken?"

"I don't feel like chicken."

"How's the veal, Gorge?" he asked the waiter for help.

"'S very nice."

"I had veal last night," she said, "and you know I don't like fish so don't suggest it."

"The curry?"

"I don't like curry. It burns my mouth."

"We could make it very mild, Madam," Gorge offered.

Harriet turned up her nose. There was an excruciating silence during which I found myself feeling sorry for Bluebeard.

A cannon exploded from across the table. "Have the steak." It was Chester Brown to the damsel in distress's rescue.

Harriet came alive. "That's what I want, a steak!" she exclaimed. "But, not so rare." She nodded to Chester in acknowledgement of his aid. "Now, why didn't you think of that?" she asked her companion who ducked his head and said, "Sorry, dear."

"I don't know why I brought you on this cruise if you can't even help me out with these simple things."

The escort mumbled "I'll try to do better" into his chest while the rest of us stared at our place settings. If Harriet had ever possessed any social inhibitions, she had sadly outgrown them.

I checked the other faces and thought I saw Old Beefy about to give her a stunning piece of his mind, but he was holding his temper.

Somehow we got through that dinner. My only other embarrassment was from the princess.

"Oh, Mr. Yates, would you do me the honor of escorting me to the show?"

I made my apologies. Tired from traveling and all.

"Come now Mr. Yates, you look like a young man to me."

"Then I look younger than I feel."

"A drink perhaps?"

"No, thank you."

She pouted in silence, but I had a feeling it wouldn't be the end of it. And the last thing I needed was someone to interfere with my single-minded goal.

I was relieved to hear Harriet and Reginald were headed for their cabin.

After a reasonable interlude, I followed. I was anxious to see if my taping system was working. Then I wanted to read the Pinkerton detective agency report on Reginald Windsor a.k.a. Fred Kantor more carefully.

Chester and Lillith left the table. Now all I had to do was shake the princess.

6

Since I didn't want to seem to be dogging Harriet and Reginald's movements, I waited at the table until they were out of sight. Seeing the two of them together was an experience. They were both short, and both had excellent posture, if ramrod is your taste. To me it looked like Harriet was trying to seem at least as tall as Reginald, who was bent on holding onto his advantage.

She appeared more self-conscious about her image, he more comfortable in his skin. It was difficult for me to imagine this little, almost gnomelike creature being anything but a little gnomelike creature. A Bluebeard? I couldn't see it. If he did kill anyone it would have had to have been a case of egregious self-defense, and then only successful because of some fluke in the proceedings. But there were *four* accidentally dead wives to his credit, and that had to be daunting.

Miss Russia was still bending my ear. If I didn't want to go to the show, how about the movie?

"No, thank you," I said. "Look here, I appreciate the attention Sophia, a lot of guys would be lucky to have you pursue them. But I *am* married."

"Well, can't we just be friends?"

I looked at those big round eyes, full of hope, and I felt a tightness in my chest.

I stood up. "Acquaintances," I said.

She stood up. I left the dining room out the back door and went up the back stairs. She followed. I ducked into the men's room. When I got out, she was waiting for me.

Unaccustomed as I am to the attention of the female of the species in my persona as Malvin Stark, I am always astonished at the swell difference when I emerge as Gil Yates.

Ordinarily I welcome the attentions of these sex fairs, but in this case I was duty-bound not to let the couple of my affections out of sight or earshot. A dalliance with this intriguing faux Russian tickled my libido and tempted me beyond good sense. I had to stay on my guard because I'm such a pushover.

I tried to smile, but failed. It wasn't that she was not attractive—she put far too much effort into the matter not to be—it was just that things were already too tense. She was studying me as though she were trying to fit me into her bed.

"You're in good shape for your age, Mr. Yates."

"Thank you," I said. Ordinarily I would have yielded to the hormone rush from such a statement. Now, I was fighting it.

"You're taller than I am, and," she added, her eyelashes fluttering, "you have such pretty blue eyes."

"Gracious goodness," I said.

"You *are* a handsome bird, in your way—"

"In my way?" Now she had piqued my interest. "What *is* my way?"

She stifled (but not too effectively) a giggle. "Oh," she said, as though she were having trouble coming up with the answer, "unthreatening, even…a little wimpy?" She said this last as though she were fishing for my acquiescence—which was definitely not forthcoming.

"Please don't follow me," I said, not unkindly, I thought.

"I just want to talk to you."

I ran up the steps. She looked after me, but didn't follow. Just to be safe, I took a jumbled route to get to my cabin without the Royal-Russian seductress on my tail.

What I didn't need was a detraction to hinder my assignment. I knew how dangerous this boy/girl stuff could be—mostly from reading a lot. I had been in what I could only call a staid marriage with a glass blower, and my exploits as Gil Yates gave me unimagined opportunities. In those cases I allowed myself to be swept off my feet, but in this circumstance it was absolutely impossible. *Verboten.*

But I could see she was not going to make it easy on me. She was playing the vamp and much to my dismay she was beginning to appeal to me. I mean, how could you hope not to be affected by someone so appealing paying you so much attention?

I was winded from the escape as I ducked into my penthouse and fell onto the bed. I took out the tape recorder and plugged in my earphones. Then I pushed the switch that gave me a live playback. There was some small-talk which seemed to me to be rather awkward. It got so tedious I reached for the Pinkerton report on Reginald and had opened its plastic cover and started to read when I heard this:

"Dear," he said. "You know I think those others at our table were a little surprised you came down on me like you did."

"Let them be."

"Did you want to tell everyone so soon and so bluntly that you were paying my way?"

"Should we hide it?"

"I guess it's up to you."

"Who pays the piper calls the tune, don't you know?"

"I guess. If your goal is to embarrass me. Is that why you brought me along, to embarrass me?"

"I just wanted you to suggest the steak. That awful man was getting special dispensation, and he's probably got a cabin in steerage."

"How do you know?"

"You can just tell by looking at him."

"So why didn't you just *say* you wanted steak?"

"I didn't want to seem like I was copying that unpleasant man."

"But you wound up copying him anyway."

"It wasn't *my* idea."

More small talk followed. In a few minutes, it got interesting again.

"So what do you think of our table mates?" Harriet asked.

"A nice enough bunch of people, I suppose." There was a silence during which I imagined her making a face. He qualified it, "I guess I'm not as fussy about people as you."

"Present company accepted?" She had a defensive edge in her voice.

"What's that?"

"When you say you aren't fussy about people, are you including *me* in that sampling? Are you with me because you aren't fussy? Then am I with *you* because I *am* fussy?"

"Oh geez Harriet, I don't know what that's all about. You know I'm crazy about you."

"But would you be if you were fussier?"

"I'd be crazy about you no matter what."

"That's better," she said.

"I take it you have reservations about our table mates?"

"Mmmm."

"Why?"

"They don't seem to have any class."

"Class? Do *I* have class?"

"When you're with me you do."

Oh my God, I thought. If this guy needs any help throwing her overboard, I'm available.

"Look at that ape for instance," she said. "I expect he has the intellect of a roto-rooter man."

"Knows how to get what he wants for dinner," he chuckled.

"That's *not* very nice," she said.

"Sorry."

"And isn't his wife's voice *aggravating?*"

"Maybe she's had an operation."

"Well this isn't a hospital! And that single woman—the one who pretends to be a Romanoff. If she's got the slightest relationship to *any* royalty, I'm Charlemagne. Isn't she an awful woman?"

"... little harsh, dear."

"The two of them, I swear. That ugly man and his beanpole with the mud-fence face, I swear we must have been saddled with the ugliest people on the ship."

"I can't comment on that," Reginald said. "There are too many mirrors in here."

"What's *that* supposed to mean?"

"I mean, I can see myself too easily to think someone else is ugly."

"You're not ugly, Reg," she reassured him. "You're a good-looking man."

He gave up arguing. I breathed a sign of relief. They seemed to have left me out of the appraisal of our table. But I had sighed too soon.

"What do you make of that single man?" she asked. "What's his name?"

"Oh, something Yates. I didn't catch his first name. Seems quiet."

"Yes, I'm afraid that faux Romanoff is going to eat him alive."

"He doesn't seem interested."

"That won't stop her. I know the type," Harriet said.

"Seems a nice enough chap, I guess. Hard to tell about people when you hardly know anything about them."

"I expect he's in steerage too."

"You don't know that."

"I know, believe me. He's alone. He wouldn't be paying forty grand to ride up here, believe you me."

"Okay—but he doesn't have to be in the cheapest cabin either."

"He is. Take my word for it. That is not a person who ever had any real money."

Alas, Reginald did not argue the point. I had to

restrain myself from knocking on their door to introduce myself as their neighbor.

Someone switched on the TV and I set the machine to record. Unfortunately the sound of the TV would keep the tape running and recording and I would have to listen to it anyway to see if anything crept through this modern form of entertainment. So I switched back to live and kept the earphones on. There were some murmurings and mutterings from their cabin, but I couldn't hear what was being said. I thought it was too early in the trip to be blasé so I kept listening in the hopes of catching something. Soon, I hoped, they would go to bed and turn off the TV.

I was fooled. They went to bed *without* turning off the TV. No doubt their TVs (two) were equipped with remote control devices just like mine were. In the meantime, I could try to focus on the Pinkerton detective report in re: Reginald Windsor.

They started with the usual disclaimers about the limited scope of the project. Implying that if the client had given them *carte blanche* and an unlimited budget they could have found more dirt. Or maybe more neutralizing information—exculpatory they called it.

The cold facts were laid out in military fashion:

SUBJECT: Reginald Windsor a.k.a. Fred Kantor, Ronald Winn, Frank Karl, Ralph Marsh, Jack Parsons
LAST KNOWN ADDRESS: (Here has listed an address in Vista, California.)
OCCUPATION: Works on and off as a tennis pro.
RACE: Caucasian
MARITAL STATUS: Multiple divorces and widowerhood
SEX: Male
HEIGHT: 5'5"
WEIGHT: 160-170 lbs.
EYE COLOR: Brown
BIRTHDATE: February 20, 1935
BIRTHPLACE: New York City
ASSIGNMENT: A background check on Reginald Windsor

was requested by Harvey Cavendish. Cavendish wishes to determine if the attentions paid by Mr. Windsor to Harvey's mother, Harriet Cavendish Jackson Whitney Lylse Himmelfarb, are of a mercenary nature. Mr. Cavendish claims to have information, the sources of which have not been disclosed, that the subject may be a confidence man who preys on single women—a man who has had multiple marriages and several wives that died of mysterious, accidental deaths. Mr. Cavendish also suspects the subject may have been prosecuted for bigamy.

METHODS: Files and records of New York State and the states of Rhode Island, Florida and California. The cities of New York, Los Angeles, Palm Springs, Newport, Palm Beach, Miami, Fort Lauderdale; Nassau County, Dade County, Los Angeles County, Broward County, Newport County, Santa Barbara County, Riverside County. Various newspapers and magazines have been used. Interviews with twenty-seven individuals with knowledge of the subject.

FINDINGS: Reginald Windsor was born Fred Kantor in the Bronx section of New York City. At the writing of this report he is using the alias Reginald Windsor. There is no record of this being a legal name change. He is, as of the date of this report, sixty-two years old. Mr. Windsor has a long history of working his way into the confidence of women, extracting large sums of money from them then disappearing, only to surface a short while later, under a different name, but often in the same locales.

Mr. Windsor is an accomplished tennis coach and has had numerous celebrity clients. Many of the people we interviewed expressed surprise that the subject chose the path he did; for he did, and could have continued to, make a good living simply giving tennis lessons. At his peak, he was earning close to $100 an hour for these lessons. It seemed to many of the interviewees that Mr. Windsor was motivated more by the challenge than by the money. We have, however, found that Reginald Windsor is a man who enjoys high living. His method is fairly standard. He meets a woman and spends a lot of money on her, impressing her with his wealth. Soon he has some story about banks tying up his funds and he, being committed to a friend for some good deed, needs a quick $25,000. His new girlfriend gives it to him and he starts over again with this windfall on another woman.

One strange aspect of his operation is we have found very few people, women or men—men have been suckered too, who will say anything bad about him. They all seemed genuinely fond of him. One interviewee, a woman from whom he took $50,000 said— "I love Jack. He has an absolute gift for making a woman feel good. I never knew a man like him. Sure I was hurt that he took the money, but, believe me, he was worth it."

The report kept on for many pages more. It chronicled his arrests for bigamy (he actually married about nine of these women as far as we know) and tax evasion. He was indicted once for murder, but never prosecuted. There have been investigations into four of his wives' deaths. But the thing that promised to make the pursuit of truth and justice so difficult in this case was no one would bad-mouth the subject. One big businessman put it this way, "Hey, I had a strong suspicion I was being conned, but what the hell—I liked the guy. If he needed the money all he had to do was ask. I'd have gladly given it to him, no questions asked."

Suddenly the sound of the television died in my earphones. There were muffled words I couldn't hear, then nondescript murmuring, then I realized what was going on and I was embarrassed. Embarrassed and ashamed to be eavesdropping on this intimacy—and amazed that it was going on at all.

But, I didn't turn off the sound.

7

The next morning we had our lifeboat drill where we all dressed in orange life jackets and piled onto our appointed deck. I was glad to have the bug so I could hear when my neighbors left their cabin. I didn't want them to think I lived close to them. Out of sight, out of mind.

Fortunately there was such a gaggle of orange-breasted penguins on the promenade deck, I could easily hide among them. When I heard my cabin number called, I didn't answer, instead telling the officer in charge when he came in my direction that I was present. I didn't see the happy couple, so I assumed they hadn't seen me.

Breakfast had been surprisingly calm between Harriet and Reginald. Princess Sophia came down after we left and Chester and Lillith had theirs on deck. So I was alone with my targets, but still playing the disinterested party. And they asked me no questions about myself so I was in no immediate danger of exposure.

Oh, I almost forgot. After all those embarrassingly intimate noises I heard the night before, Reginald was extravagant in his verbal endearments directed to his companion. She was gracious in her acceptance of the praise, but didn't give any in return.

At lunch we had the whole troop. Fortunately, I was able to sit apart from the princess. I was the second last to arrive and the other couples had left one seat between them on each side of the table. Terribly thoughtful, I thought, and I nodded and smiled my acknowledgement and appreciation as I sat down. I noticed a returned half-smile from Chester and a twinkle from Reginald. I expected this would have been a boys' operation.

When the princess sashayed into the room and sat down, she didn't take her eyes off me the whole time.

Nothing much developed at the meal, though I did hear Lillith refer to her husband as Chesty. I thought that a most apt nickname because, in addition to outsized thighs and buttocks, Chesty Brown had an enormous chest. None of him, however, was shaped in a conventional fashion, and he didn't look like Mr. America, but rather a gorilla with a bottom at each end.

Star-struck Sophia continued to stare while she ordered and while she ate her salad. She didn't speak a word, and blessedly did not follow me when I left the table.

When I returned to my cabin, I noticed the stewardess had mounted six of my palm and cycad pictures on the mirror in front of the desk. She had pushed them into the frames of the mirror at eye level (when I was sitting down). Given more time to brood, I could have become homesick.

She had put up my *Brahea armata,* and the silver-blue color of this unique palm looked stunning, if I do say so myself. On the other side was the large *Encephalartos hildebrandtii*—a cycad that I paid so much for with my first fee. The triangle palm *Neodypsis decaryii* was there, and I was reminded the *Butia capitata* was growing so well. I had a picture of a bunch of new *Livistonas,* but they were pretty small. I liked to take pictures of my palms at year-or-so intervals to note the progress.

Now if I could only make some progress on the Himmelfarb matter.

Then I got a break.

I had put on the earphones, but while I was ogling my palm pictures, I was oblivious to the goings on next door. When I came back to earth, I noticed what was going on was that nothing was going on. I heard water running in the sink, but no voices. One person was in, I decided, one out. Switching the device back to record, I left the cabin in search of one or the other of them who did not return.

Our section of the ship had five penthouses—and it was sealed off with a glass door at the end of the corridor. The door had decals on each side. One said PUSH, the other PULL. Even so, I had difficulty getting it right. While I was in this small corridor, I was always afraid one of them would see me and get suspicious, though suspicious of what, I couldn't tell.

Outside the corridor, on the other side of the PULL door was a vestibule with two elevators. I always took the stairs so I wouldn't run into Reg or Harriet. Ordinarily, I did not want to see them in any proximity to the cabin. But now I was looking for one of them, somewhere, anywhere.

On the main deck three white-haired women in wheelchairs were waiting for the elevator. A man with clear plastic tubes in his nose was rounding the bend pulling an oxygen tank on wheels. The top of the tank came up to his knee cap and was the size of his thigh.

I checked all the public rooms on the floor: the library, the gift shop specializing in beaded dresses and over-priced jewelry, the photo shop where the walls were adorned with pictures of people boarding. I had slipped a fiver to the photographer, a most attractive young woman, in apology for not having my picture taken. She seemed pleased.

I got sidetracked looking at the pictures in search of my table mates. I saw the princess first—she was alone showing some of her Chopin teeth in a smile. The svelte body was sheathed in some provocative purple goods that aroused the imagination.

Chesty and Lillith looked like a couple who knew all the tricks of cruising, but standing side by side they looked an unlikely pair. He, with his oversized, slouching body had the look of a prize fighter who had been stunned by a blow to the nose. She had her perpetual smile, her little-girl naïveté on that galvanized-nail body.

But seeing Harriet and Reginald was a revelation. Harriet stared straight into the camera with a vengeance, lest that instrument of recorded doom catch her in an unflattering profile that would show her hunchbacked nose.

Reginald was not afraid of his profile and while Harriet stared straight ahead as though she were in the shot alone, Reginald looked worshipfully at her. The profile gave the impression his head was cut in half with black hair on the back half from the ear up, and white skin on the front half. He looked very happy. She looked guarded.

From the photo shop, I went to the big lounge in back. A dance class was in progress, and I didn't see anyone I knew. I went through a corridor full of bridge players, through the shops and the casino. I didn't see anyone. I realized one of them could have been taking a nap, or we could have passed somewhere—one of them on the elevator while I was on the stairs, or en route where I was not. As a last shot before I returned to the cabin I went out on the promenade deck, where the sign told me each lap was a quarter mile, and then, as though the math were too tough, underneath it told us four laps equaled a mile. As people were coming at me I felt as though I were trapped in some octogenarian Olympics, and I fell in with the flow only to be passed up again and again by one aggressor after another. This, I decided, was not the place to find Harriet *or* Reginald. I was about to admit defeat and return when I sold myself on an investment of a quarter mile, especially since I realized this exercise had the calorie-busting equivalent of a couple of cooked carrots.

As I rounded the stern turn where the paddle tennis court held a man and a woman having a battle to the death, I saw Reginald in a deck chair watching the game.

"Reginald," I exclaimed. "How's it going?"

"Great," he said. He was always the optimist. "You look a little pooped, want to sit down?"

I looked at the deck chair beside him with the inviting blue and white striped pad sprawled seductively across it—as though nothing could have been further from my mind at the moment.

"Well," I said. "Well, yeah, sure, I guess so." and having set the surprise up I flopped down.

"Been hitting the deck?"

"Yeah, if you hadn't stopped me, I'da made a quarter

of a mile, easy."

He laughed.

"I'm not what you'd call a world-class athlete," I said. "You?"

"Naw," he said. "Did a little tennis awhile back."

"Oh, yeah—that why you're sitting here?"

"I guess. Partially," he said. "To tell the truth, Harriet gave me a hundred bucks to bet in the Casino. I lost it so fast I was embarrassed to go up so soon, so I'm killing a little time."

His eyes were on the netted court in front of us. The netting must have been ten feet high on all four sides to keep the tennis balls from flying into the ocean. Even so, they seemed to lose a few. I could just imagine some guy marooned on a raft coming upon floating tennis balls. Then I considered the mathematical chances and decided there was *no* danger of it happening.

"She's pretty good," Reginald said, his eyes following the ball.

I looked at the match and decided while she was "pretty good," the guy was lots better. I guess Reg didn't have an eye for the fellas like he did for the ladies. And this was no beauty queen, but a hefty, broad-boned frau with piano legs and hamhock arms who would never see fifty again.

Carefully, I said, "He looks better to me."

"Well, of course. Men are usually better. Bigger, stronger, it's a given. I just don't spend a lot of time watching men. I prefer women."

"A-men," I said, to be one of the boys. "Said you played?"

"Little," he said. "Used to teach it, actually."

"Really? Professionally?"

He nodded with a whiff of nostalgia.

"Why'd you give it up?"

"Judge," he said.

"You gave it up to judge matches?"

"No. It was the judge's idea."

"Judge? A tennis judge? You hit someone or something?" My wife would say playing stupid was only typecasting for me.

"No, a criminal judge. Got in a lot of hot water with my coaching. Went to jail for a spell."

"For coaching tennis?" I pumped out the incredulity. "You teach someone wrong or something?"

"Nah—borrowed some money, didn't pay it back. You don't want to hear my life story, believe me," he said.

I shrugged the maximum disinterest I could shrug. "I don't know. I got a lot of time. What is it, about nine more days till we see land?"

He laughed. "Yeah, and it would take that long to tell it, too," he said.

"Well, why don't you start? I'll turn you off if I get bored."

"Oh, you wouldn't get bored. My life has been anything but boring. I just wouldn't know where to start."

"How about why a judge won't let you play tennis?"

"Funny thing," he said, wistfully watching this paddle tennis game in front of us. "The conditions of my parole include I can't go within twelve-hundred feet of a tennis court."

"What? Really? Geez, are you in violation of your parole now?"

"Could be," he said, "but I'd argue this was *paddle tennis,* not the real thing. Besides anywhere on the ship I'm within twelve hundred feet of the court. The ship isn't that long." He laughed a belly-deep, jowl-shaking jovial laugh that puffed up his features in a melancholy way.

"I still don't understand why a judge would care if you played tennis or not," I said. "Are you allowed to play golf?"

"Didn't say anything about golf. Thought it was tennis got me in trouble. Used to earn almost a hundred an hour."

"That sounds good to me."

"I guess it was, but it was never enough for me. I

44

figure I got what you'd call a sickness."

"Oh? What kind?"

"The making-women-happy sickness. Especially unhappy women and women who've never really been happy. You be surprised at how many women have never been happy. Never had anyone care about 'em. No one ever done anything nice for them, even just listened to their troubles."

"So why should that get you in trouble?"

"Shouldn't," he readily agreed. "But I got this thing, see, it's not enough to just make *one* happy, I've got to keep moving."

Wow, I thought, here he is laying out a warning already. The woman playing paddle tennis missed a shot and said to her more elderly male partner, "How do you expect me to return them from the corner?" Was *she* happy? I wondered.

"Not this time," Reginald said, as though he had read my mind. "This time's special. I'm hooked."

I didn't want to question that yet. Better it comes voluntarily from him. Let him admit his past first. "So they arrested you for moving on to another woman?"

"Ah," he said waving his hand at me, "it's too complex. You really wouldn't be interested."

"No, I really am," I said. "So how do you go about making these women happy? I'd really like to know that."

"That's my problem. Luxury. I got to do everything in style. Limos, best restaurants, best wines, expensive jewelry. I got to lay on that I'm a wealthy man. I don't know why—all of them say it wouldn't make any difference—but I guess it's inferiority or something makes me want to be rich. You know, like why else would a woman want to have anything to do with a fat, bald, funny-looking man if he didn't have bucks?"

"I don't know," I said. "I think the real women are more interested in the down-to-earth stuff. What I hear, anyway. I still don't understand how any of this gets you in trouble with the law."

"Where and how I get the money."

"How do you?" I hoped I sounded as low key and objective as I thought I did.

"I'm a con, basically," he said, as though he were telling me what time the next bus were due. "Soon as I get money from one, I'm off to the next. I can't explain it, it's some kind of need I guess. I *do* love the women. I love them all. I just love women, so there's nothing phony about it. I'm genuine," he said, as though that were absolution enough. "But in the past I could never be satisfied to please just one woman. The money they gave me, I guess that was just the icing on the cake. Like that was when I knew I had succeeded in pleasing them, when they were willing to trust me with their life savings."

"Hey, I just thought of something," I said. "How about working your magic on Sophia, Princess Romanoff?"

"Hey, she isn't really a princess is she?" he asked, and I thought I noted a momentary flicker of interest.

"Of course not, but would it make a difference?"

"Would have in the past. You bet your life."

"Past?"

"It's different now. Doesn't appeal. Afraid she's going to be *your* cross on this cruise."

"Worth a try," I shrugged. "But why is it different now?"

"Oh, I don't know," he said, "it just is. I'm older for one thing—I'm over sixty. I can't keep the pace, and I don't fancy going back to the slammer."

"Slammer. You've been in?" I said, then I remembered he had said "Conditions of my parole." He didn't seem bothered by my lapse of memory.

"Sure I have. It doesn't always work. Sometimes they prosecute. But if they do it's because of their pride. I wounded it. But other than wounded pride, I never had anyone bad-mouth me. All agreed I'd been nicer to them than anyone before. And some of these women had been married five or six times when I got to them. Through the mill, a lot of them, and never really knew a man that cared about them like I did. I was filling a need."

"But holy geez—jail. I mean, how *was* that?"

"Could have been worse. They don't put the con artists with the axe murderers, you know. And in the hierarchy inside, us cons are at the top of the heap. Lot of respect. At bottom are the child molesters and everything else is in between."

"Whew, I'm just knocked out," I said as a wild-eyed innocent. "You just don't look the type."

"Oh no? What type do I look?"

"Oh, maybe an orthopod man, or a CEO of a thriving midsized manufacturing company." I was pretty proud of those answers and the pride it gave him. Conning a con was most satisfying.

"You flatter me," he said easily, but there was no argument from either of us.

The paddle tennis players left the court and Reginald watched the woman until she was out of sight. Come to think of it, she was built a little like my wife and I had a momentary pause wondering how Tyranny Rex would respond to a guy like Reg.

"Are you enjoying the cruise so far?" I decided to shift to calmer waters. I had to admit I had been won over by this show of frankness and willingness of a stranger to open his heart, admit his faults, his denigrating past. I just thought we could both use a breather.

"Sure, love it," then he frowned. "Except for that incident last night at the table. I don't know why she does that. Fills a need, I guess, to put me down. When we're alone she's quite loving."

"You don't have to answer this, but isn't she a lot older than you?"

"Nah, not a lot," he said. "She's only seventy-six—so what's that? Fourteen years? Nothing."

"Well, I was a little shocked at her saying that, I'll admit. My take on the thing was she should be very grateful to have you."

"No, no, I'm the lucky one. She *is* taking me. What do I have to offer? I'm an ex-con and a bigamist in the bargain."

"A *bigamist*?" I sounded alarmed. "Does she know that?"

"Oh sure, I've told her everything. Clean breast. Like Alcoholics Anonymous, I never shut up about my failed past."

"You took a twelve-step cure?"

"Something like that. Couple steps, anyway."

"And she accepts all this? I mean *bigamy*! That's really heavy."

"Yeah," he said. "A couple times."

"Twice?"

"Well," he dropped his head sheepishly, "more like three."

"Oh man."

"Well, I got caught up. If marriage was what it took to make them happy, I married them."

"Yeah, but all at once?"

"Yeah, well there was some overlapping."

"Are you married now?"

"Oh, no. Last one was a divorce, clean and simple."

"Did *that* make her happy?

"Guess not, but there's no animosity. She accepts it and even said it would save her a lot of money."

"She was rich?"

"My daddy *always* said it was as easy to love them rich as it was to love them poor."

"And was it?"

"Far's I'm concerned," he sighed. "Last one even settled a little money on me. Just so's I could get my feet on the ground before my next score, was how she put it."

"And Harriet is your next score?"

"Not a score, no. Harriet is the real thing. Just between us, I'd like to marry her."

He must have read the thoughts on my tortured face.

"'How can that be?' you are probably saying. Well, I'll tell you. She's generous and kind. She was an only child of a very rich man, but she admits she was spoiled. She wouldn't say these tactless things otherwise. She knows she does it and she's sorry for it, but she's had five other husbands and nobody could touch what I do for her."

"And what is that—what you do for her?"

"I love her. She's a terrific lover."

"At seventy-six?"

"You bet. I bolster her self-esteem. I'm a genial companion—women get lonely without men, you know. It's a validation of their self-worth to have a man around."

The sun was flaming out on the horizon and our thoughts were turning to another gluttonous meal.

"So, what's Harriet's reaction to your marriage proposal?"

"Oh, I haven't made it yet. I thought this ship would be a good place. What do you think?"

"Well, I, yeah. I don't know, why not?" I found myself in the ridiculous position of encouraging him.

The ship was gently rocking and the sun had spilled some melted butter on the water. It was a pleasant sensation.

"I think she'll accept. I hope she will anyway. I'm ready to settle down."

"So what reservations are you expecting from Harriet?"

"Oh, just the money thing. Her kid is scared to death she's going to give all her dough to me. Cut him and his sister out."

"What does Harriet think?"

"She thinks Harvey is a crybaby, but she also thinks what with my background and all, we should consider, if we ever are serious about getting married—we should maybe do one of those prenuptial agreements."

"Would you sign that?"

"Oh, absolutely," he said, bobbing his bald head enthusiastically. "I'm nuts about her."

8

I bade Reg goodbye by the paddle tennis court and let him get back to the cabin before I started back. I sat there in that deck chair looking out at our expiring sun and wondering about what I just heard.

It all seemed so refreshingly candid. Almost too refreshingly candid. I was beginning to wonder if Reg was setting me up, conning me maybe, so that I could be a witness or an alibi or a fall guy—or worse, did he suspect my role and was just playing me for a sucker?

The next few days passed uneventfully. My earphones and tape recorder yielded little but mundane conversations through the walls. There was close to zero communication between Reginald and Harriet that could be termed intellectual. He was unfailingly solicitous of her comfort and pleasure, complimentary about her clothes, her hairdos, her general appearance. She was cordial and circumspect. There were no girly giggles from her, no age-inappropriate behavior.

I could see why women were crazy about him. He put them and their wishes first. He seemed to idolize her, a difficult object for idolatry.

It could not be surprising that women found his behavior unusual and endearing.

But I could also understand why Reginald moved quickly from one relationship to another. It was not the sort of behavior anyone would be able to keep up for any length of time.

Our conversations at dinner were moving into the less guarded phase. Of course, unguarded conversation has a precipitous downside. I, personally, do not cherish the let-it-all-hang-out school of discourse. A lot of stuff hangs out that would be so much better trussed up. I realize that is easy for me to say because the stuff I wanted to hang out from the Harriet/Reginald axis was being bugged by my little machine.

At the table, tidbits began to drop from the sensual red mouth of the faux Russian, revealing hints of a less-than-idyllic past. Mysterious addictions, mean men, the usual.

Chesty's food orders were excruciatingly unvaried. "Steak! *Rare!* Don't bring it well done. And fries and catsup—and hold the vegetables. And A.1. sauce! And I want my coffee with my steak. Always!"

I rarely said anything at mealtime. There was so little opportunity, and it was just as well. Imagine the reaction if I talked about my newest cycad, an *Encephalartos ghellinckii,* or the palm I got from Lord Howe Island that no one knows how to classify.

Chesty took a lot of the floor time to expound his political principles which were not at odds with the philosophy of cruising. They were political ideas that I could identify with, and might have at one time considered my own, but hearing them come from the booming basso˙of Old Beefy they seemed stiflingly elitist. Now, I never thought there was anything wrong with elitism, provided it was espoused by the elite. Hearing this bozo promote these ideas seemed gauche.

George Bernard Shaw once said, "The government that robs Peter to pay Paul always meets with the approval of Paul." But if this guy Chesty is Peter, sign me up with the Pauls.

The old ship (not so old really—about five years to be precise) was rocking and rolling on the Pacific. But it was a nice lullaby motion, like someone had a very gentle foot on the cradle. It was conducive to calm.

I guess I am a naive sort, but it took me several days to realize that Harriet was partial to the sauce. A lot of that little-girl defensiveness came from her inebriation.

It was the fourth day at sea when during an uncharacteristic lull in the dinner conversation, Reginald gave us a hypothetical: "Boy, I stare over that railing on the deck and see all that water and nothing else day after day. I wonder how many people have the feeling I do."

"What feeling?" Lillith asked him.

"The feeling that if I don't control myself I'll jump over. Any of you experience that?" he asked, his eyes circling the table.

The silence that followed seemed somewhat shocked.

Sophia raised her hand halfway up. "I have," she said.

"Well I hope *you* won't jump," Harriet said to Reginald, "I'd miss you—"

"Thank you, dear," he said, and the subject was changed.

I thought about that for a long time. What was he trying to accomplish? Did he want to set us up for Harriet's disappearance at sea? Was he going to stage a fake disappearance to get out of it himself? Did he want to set up a fake double suicide with her going to the bottom and him going to the bank?

But why would he need her dead at all? With a million a year to spend, a guy could put up with a lot of aggravation. But that was not Reginald's style. Reginald took the money and ran. What was it they said about teaching an old mutt new routines?

And maybe Reginald learned a lesson in his varied career as a con man; a lesson I should have committed to memory early on in my relationship with Tyranny Rex's father, Daddybucks: Ability to pay is no sign of willingness to pay.

It was the night of the captain's reception, that touching time when all the paying customers get to pay obeisance to the captain of the ship, the guy who draws his tax-free stipend (the ocean collects no taxes) from the happy vacationers. The captain in his turn makes believe he is happy as a clam to meet you while the ship's photographer takes a shot of you shaking the big man's hand, only to offer you a copy later for $5.45.

I waited a few seconds after I heard Reginald and Harriet leave for the captain's party. Then, I strolled to the public room where the cap was holding forth and they were passing out the canapés and the schnapps without sticking it on your bill.

I shook the smiling captain's hand and he said he was pleased to meet me and I allowed as how I was pleased to meet him too while the flash bulb flashed its instant burst of yellow on the room. I took a drink of Evian water and a tortured shrimp on a circular piece of bread that for some stupid reason reminded me of a communion wafer, and moseyed over to my two pals.

Harriet was holding a drink that looked like water but wasn't. Reginald had something with an amber hue.

"Ho, Yates," he said, as I passed by them. I made believe I was headed for somewhere else and just happened to pass by. Looking back, all this fancy footwork was probably not necessary but you know what they say: A stitch in time can save an awful lot of sewing later on.

"Well, Reginald. How's it going?"

"Aren't you going to say hello to me?" Harriet petitioned me in her defensive posture.

"Oh, sorry, Harriet, of course. I guess I didn't notice you there behind this big guy."

"He's not *that* big," she said. "Sometimes I feel you are ignoring me."

"Well, I'm really sorry. I don't intend to. I guess I'm just pretty out of it sometimes. You know, my mind on other things. I'll try to do better."

"Well, pal, that was okay in my book," Reginald said. "A very nice recovery don't you think, dear?"

Her nose turned up. "I *guess* so," she said, leaving the door open for more convincing, but I didn't have it in me.

"Well, Harriet," I said, addressing the attention to her, "I'm glad to see your friend hasn't given into the urge to jump overboard."

"So am *I*," she said. "I'd miss him."

"Would you jump too?"

"No! I *don't* share that urge."

The waiter paused, and she took a glass of champagne from his tray. Her other glass was still a quarter full.

"Would you jump over to save him?"

"How could I do that? Would I still be alive after I hit the water?"

"Good question," I said. "I don't really know."

"I think I could do better by screaming for them to stop the boat."

We ground out some smaller talk, Harriet had another gin and tonic and then we went to dinner. She was pretty well sloshed by then, and I noticed the meanness surface. But Reginald was a master at deferring to her moods. So when she turned up her nose at the menu, he immediately suggested the steak. Before she could clap her hands and say goodie that's just what I want, old beefy croaked "That's what I'm having. Steak! *Rare!*" and she changed her mind.

Reginald finally satisfied her by asking the captain to make her pasta, table side. She basked in the attention.

After dinner, we went to the show. It was the singers and dancers that went with the ship in a show about a bunch of countries. When they got to Holland, the girls bent over and flipped their skirts over their heads and stood up, and they were tulips—green tights for the stems and red, pink and yellow petals for the flowers. It brought down the house. These dancers were sensational with bodies to die for, but I thought I might live awhile longer.

Harriet polished off three more drinks before she staggered, on the arm of Reginald, back to her cabin.

In mine, with the earphones on, I got alarmed when I heard the following:

"Why don't I draw a bath for you?"

"Oh, that would be nice."

And then I heard the water running.

One of Reginald's wives had drowned in the bathtub. The coroner had ruled it an accidental drowning due to the high alcohol level in her blood.

9

Unfortunately, I couldn't make out the words from the bathroom with the water running. The bug worked best when my neighbors were in the sleeping and living portion of the penthouse. I had not considered the bathroom area as one of conversation.

I was perspiring, my forehead had droplets and my armpits were wet. I didn't know what to do. Should I knock on their door and ask to borrow a bar of soap? It would blow my proximity, and I couldn't knock on the door every time I heard the water running. On the other hand if I didn't do *something*, there might not be a next time. And if I didn't bring her back alive there would be no fee for me. I don't want to appear mercenary, but I am in this hobby business for the money, not for knighthood.

So I sat there with those earphones pasted to my wet head, concentrating on the sound of running water, racking my brain to try to remember how long it took me to fill the bathtub. I hastened to make what I call panic plans. Those are the plans I make to avoid panic in crises. The trouble is, I don't often make them before I am already in a state of panic. Like now. You would expect to reason so much more rationally *before* you panic.

Well, I didn't, so I was panicked and trying to reason, which is not easy to do when I am panicked.

Possibilities: (1) It was all my imagination. She was simply taking a bath. (2) He was drowning her right this minute. It should be easy for him to hold her head under for the couple minutes it would take, *while* the water was running. Then he would leave the water running, slip out of the room, and go to the casino and make it known that he was there, perhaps with a $100 tip to the dealer. (3) Or this could be a wet run for the real thing.

Afraid I wouldn't hear him slip out with the water running, I opened my cabin door. The cabin doors made that nice clicking noise when they opened, and there was a hefty slam when they closed. Reginald might defeat the slam by easing the door closed, but he could do nothing to muffle the telltale click of the locking mechanisms slipping in and out of place.

Had he already slipped out? Could he have accomplished all he needed to in that short time?

I thought if the water ran much longer I could telephone their room. If no one answered I'd call the steward to check, under what pretense I didn't know yet. Another blow struck for doing panic planning *before* you panic. On the other hand, I didn't want to cry fox. I might need these people later, and I wouldn't want them dismissing me in a real crisis as an alarmist.

Then the sound of running water ceased. I listened carefully for voices but heard nothing. But someone must have been alive in there to turn off the water. I sharpened my ears. He had drowned her while the water was running, and now he would slip out for a long night at the casino. But the door didn't open. I would call and if no one answered I would reason he had already begun his alibi. If someone answered I would just hang up.

As I picked up the phone I heard the unmistakable upper-crust voice in my earphones "Wash my back, dear."

"Yes, dear," was the response. I dropped the phone and exhaled a ton of anxieties. Then I closed my door.

Before I knew it, she was out of the tub, and I heard her say—"Dry me, honey." Then they came closer to my hidden microphone and it was his voice saying "Commere darling," and she came to him, and then it was those embarrassing intimate noises all over again: the coos and ooos, the ohs and ahs, the extravagant praise from Reginald for Harriet's exquisite beauty, the depth of his love for her, the whole bit.

Then I thought how foolish I had been. The sequence was all wrong. Why would he kill her now? What could he gain? They weren't married, he wouldn't get a farthing. No, I decided the time to start the panicking was when they got married. Of course, I couldn't be with them every minute, but I didn't see where they had had the opportunity to get married either. I had no hint of anything until the next formal dinner.

I noticed the women on board loved these formal nights; they could play dress-up and adorn themselves with all kinds of finery that would never see the illumination of day in the real world. I always got a kick out of the routine: the designers, most of whom were not, as we say nowadays, oriented toward women, who if we analyzed it, might even have a built-in aversion to women; these designers were dressing women for these "formal" occasions.

But the women loved to dress up. The men for these "formal" events dressed in drab, meld-into-the-background black to act as foils for the female finery. So the finery begot the events, not the other way around. Women, loving to dress in costumes so extravagant as to be unsuitable for ordinary wear, promoted these formal events as an opportunity to show off their dresses in public.

Cruising offered *beaucoup* opportunities for dress up. And when it did, the ship's beauty shop was booked solid, for on these occasions no aid to beautifying the female of the species, no matter how far gone in years, was too far-fetched. On these evenings, the birds fanned their feathers, and they paraded through the dining room with their drapery dresses, their bouffant hair, freshly colored, combed and upswept, the tinted beehives, the jewelry glimmering in the electric lighting, not so harsh as to rob their cosmetic beauty with glare, but just enough to set the diamonds sparkling.

Tyranny Rex was not immune to the charms of dressing up. So I had a tuxedo in my possession. Some of the guys on the ship wore dark suits on these happy occasions, but all of us took the oath to let the women shine.

Reginald, with Harriet's approval, had succumbed to the fifty-eight-dollar-a-bottle wine to go with the filet mignon on the menu. And, as expected, Harriet got slightly tipsy.

Our table was representative of the ship. Reginald and I wore tuxes. Chesty had on a blue suit that was almost dark. His wife was in a pink knit floor-length dress, simple and elegant. Harriet wore a floor-length, black chiffon thing that had rhinestones wrapped around the bodice.

But the prize winner for the most daringly original concoction of the evening went to our very own Sophia Romanoff, the princess. She was in something deep apricot that I hesitate to call a dress because I'm not an expert. It looked like a mile of shiny drapery fabric. It was wrapped and folded, blown out and tucked in; the rounded goods atop her respectable legs made her look like a tantalizing candy apple, good enough to eat.

When the dessert came, Reginald hoisted his glass and smiled from ear to ear and back again. "Attention please," he said. "I have an announcement to make."

"Oooo" cooed Princess Romanoff.

"What kinda announcement?" boomed Old Beefy.

"I've never been happier in my life than I have been on this cruise with Harriet, my sweetie. I would like to take this opportunity among dear friends to ask her for her hand in marriage." Appropriate exclamations of delight followed.

"Oh you flatterer," Harriet said. "Don't you say the nicest things!"

"So are you saying yes?" Beefy wanted to know.

"Well, I'm going to give it very serious thought," she said. And all the others seemed disappointed.

I was relieved.

10

Back in the cabin, I threw on the earphones and listened to the discussion already in progress. I'm sure it began on the way back, but I have no way of knowing what was said.

"...You don't mean you are rejecting me, do you?" it was Reginald's voice.

"No, I'm not saying that, darling. It's just we have so much to consider."

"I love you, Honeycakes, so why should we put off being together for the rest of our lives?"

"That could be a long time," she said. Tipsy as she seemed at the table, she must have sobered up. I was pulling for her.

"But not long enough," he said. And I'll say this for him, he seemed to mean it. "I've never felt like this before," he said.

"We've both made a lot of mistakes with the opposite sex in our lives," she said, "don't you know? I for one don't wish to make another."

"Me neither. But I was another person then. I'm not even using the same name now. I want a clean break from that sordid past. I want you, now, babe, nothing else. Nobody ever gave me the pleasure you do, Honeycakes—I just love being with you."

There was a respectable pause in the conversation.

"What do you say?" Reginald prodded Harriet.

"I say Harvey would kill me."

"Your son? Why?"

"Harvey said he'd like a prenuptial agreement," she said, quietly.

"Fine!" he said. "I'll sign anything you want. Why don't we make it up right now?"

"I wouldn't know how to go about it. It might not be legal."

Oh, was my estimation of Harriet Himmelfarb skyrocketing!

"Well, let's just write and sign anything you want." Reginald said, "and when we get back we'll have a lawyer redo it. Anything you want, Honeycakes, really. I'm easy."

"But why are you changing all of a sudden?"

"I'm sixty-two going on sixty-three—I don't have these stupid needs anymore—the glamour stuff—the limos and jewels. I've finally outgrown it all. And I never felt so relieved of a burden. Why don't we just sign a simple statement that Harvey shall inherit all your money."

After another silence, she said. "Let me think about it."

It was followed by a resonant, smacking kissing sound.

After lunch the next day, following the lovers, I noticed Harriet reached into her purse and withdrew some good old greenbacks and handed them to Reginald who bowed with exaggerated gratitude while Harriet lectured him in her patented fashion—head tilted back, looking down (or across) her sharp bumpy nose.

I followed Reginald to the casino. Harriet stopped in the adjoining Oak Room and ordered a drink.

Sophia, our princess, was standing at the door of the casino looking in—I thought rather wistfully.

Reginald strode purposefully past her, his mind focused on his destination at a blackjack table across the room. He didn't acknowledge our tablemate.

He seemed the only man on the ship who could look the other way in the presence of our princess. The men hung on her like flies on high-fructose corn syrup.

Sophia was looking so forlornly into the casino, I couldn't bring myself to ignore her as Reginald had.

"Well, Sophia," (I was careful to say So-*fee*-ah), "you going to make a donation to the ship today?" I tossed my head toward the casino.

"Oh," she said, as though embarrassed to be caught at something forbidden. "No," she said, and turned abruptly. "Gambling is my poison," she smiled bleakly and walked away.

I watched Reginald become part of the casino, with its rows of electronic slot machines, its crap table and two blackjack tables, one with a man dealing to two participants, the other with the woman dealer sitting alone leafing through a magazine. Reginald glided to the table with the woman dealer. She smiled at him as he put out his arm toward the chair, obviously asking if he could sit there and play. She seemed happy for the company, and began to shuffle the cards.

Several older women and a man were pushing the buttons of the machines next to the wall. I was surprised to see none of them were smiling. If gambling were fun, why did this seem such a grim business? Then I noticed Reginald had taken up his blackjack cards and he was smiling. We might have been in for a long day.

Harriet was sitting in the Oak Room where she had already obtained a vodka and tonic which was sitting in front of her on the small, low chrome-legged table topped with smoke glass. A little swizzle stick in the glass pointed up to her like a beacon of shining light at the grand opening of some used car lot. Harriet was not a car, true, but sitting there alone in this macho-decor men's saloon, she did look used.

"Well, Mr. Yates," she proclaimed in her little dictator manner, "I don't suppose you'd join me in a drink. You don't approve of drinking!" and she punctuated the statement with a pucker of her face.

I sat quickly before the invitation could be withdrawn. "Where did you get that idea?"

"You don't drink, do you?"

"No, but I don't pass judgment either," I said meekly. "So, what are you doing about the burning question of the cruise?" I asked.

She smiled as the cat who had swallowed the canned fairy. "I'm thinking," she said, adding a teasing wink.

"Thinking pro or con?"

"He's a nice man," she said, sipping her booze, "I do like being with him, and from my vantage point that's the most important thing. I know from experience I'm not always that easy to be with, so I'm lucky from that standpoint. But..." she sighed and trailed off.

I waited. She took another sip. I noticed for the first time quite a little went down the hatch with those sips.

"There are a lot of differences between us, don't you see?" It may have been my imagination, but I thought she cranked up the British inflections when she began talking of differences.

"How different?" I asked.

"*My* ancestors came over on the Mayflower," she said, as though that explained everything. I didn't mention the well-mauled suspicion that if a tiny fraction of the claimed ancestral Mayflower passengers really rode the old tub, it either made an awful lot of trips or it would have sunk before it left the dock. I would hope that if she were to throw up this canard to Reginald he would say "My family came later, they sent their servants on the Mayflower." Lord, how many "genealogists" made a fortune tying families to the Mayflower? Often with an eight- to twelve-generation gap, but I didn't question Harriet. I didn't want her to marry him, after all.

"His folks missed the boat?" I asked her.

"In a *big* way. They came over the generation he was born to. And from *Poland*," she said, putting on that sour face again, which no one could do better.

"Poland?" I said, shocked. "Windsor is a *Polish* name?"

"Of course, not," she said, "he changed it. It was Kantor. He's *Jewish!*" she said. "My ancestors would roll over in their graves!"

"Why?"

"Well in *those* days it was *declassé* to date a Jewish man."

Date? I thought. What a happy choice of words. "Well, fortunately we're over that," I said.

"Oh, don't be too sure. A lot of my friends turn up their noses when they see the size of *his* nose. *Reginald Windsor* or no!"

"Well, it's good *you* don't feel that way."

"But that's just it. I *do* sometimes," she said. "Then there are all the terminated marriages we have had between us—fourteen in all. Do we really need to do that again?"

She went on to tell me quite candidly about all the stuff in the Pinkerton report.

"Would you like another drink?" I asked.

"Yes, I would."

The waiter came right over. He had anticipated her wish and set down before her a fresh vodka and tonic.

"I like vodka because it doesn't make your breath smell," she explained.

"Does he, I mean, he certainly doesn't admit killing any of his wives, does he?"

"Oh, no. Says they're all accidents. Makes him extra solicitous of me. Anytime I get near the edge of anything he gets nervous and pulls me back."

I thought, what a nice set up. She'll trust him and one day, instead of pulling, he'll push.

"He watches me in the bathtub every minute so I won't slip."

"That's nice."

"I think so," she said.

"So you aren't afraid if you marry him, you'll have a sudden bad accident?"

"Oh, no, not Reginald, he's a lamb. Besides, he inherited money from the others. He wouldn't from me."

"How come?"

"Harvey, my son, insists I make a prenuptial agreement so he and his sister will get their mitts on the money. I've talked it over with Reginald. He's agreeable to anything."

"He seems like a very agreeable sort," I agreed.

"He *is*," she emphasized.

"So you *are* going to marry him?"

"I'm still thinking. My son, Harvey, thinks it's foolish for a seventy-six year old, married five times, to think about it again. But all my marriages were long. Well, all but one, and another who died. I was married to Harvey's father for almost twenty years. After we divorced I had my rebound marriage, a huge mistake. He was a crazy. Lasted just under two years which seemed like ten years too long.

"Then I married the General, and he died in less than a year."

"What from?"

"An accident. He fell in the tub. He drank a lot and was getting so old. That's something we have in common," she said.

"What?"

"We both lost spouses to bathtub accidents."

Wow. From now on when I heard the bath water run, I wouldn't know whom to worry about.

"Then the doctor. We had almost nine good years before he died in a car crash."

"Drinking?"

"I am afraid so. They think he might have had a heart attack at the wheel. The car crashed into a telephone pole. Maybe he was asleep," she sighed at the memory. "My last husband lived four years after we married. But he was old. He was almost ninety when he died."

Now I was beginning to wonder. Did she have a hand in any of those demises?

She read my mind. "I didn't get much money from

any of them. My money's from my father."

"So, do you think you'll marry Reginald?"

"Possibly," she said. "If I could only win Harvey over. I know, I'm a grown woman. Reginald says I raised that boy and he hasn't been too grateful. Likes to feel sorry for himself because of the divorce. Likes to blame all his troubles on me."

"What are his troubles?"

"He never amounted to much on his own. He's jealous of his sister and her husband's success."

"So what do you want him to get—half the money?"

"I guess I should start thinking about it," she said. "Maybe he'd be better off without a farthing."

In a way, her talking about her son sounded like she was talking about Reginald. I was put in mind of those circle clichés, like, what goes around comes back, or something like that. Then there is that Pennsylvania Dutch saying:

"The more we go the world about
The more we find bejesus out."

What I am getting at is, here she is, attracted to a man who shares her son's weaknesses. But, the son must have gotten them somewhere.

"What was Harvey's father like?" I asked.

"A lot like Harvey, actually," Harriet said. "He was always looking for the big, easy dollar. His second wife was rich, but after she died he blew it all, and now the easy money continues to elude him."

"Gee," I said. "This sounds familiar."

She nodded. "When you've lived as long as I have, you keep seeing repeats of what you've already experienced, don't you see? I suppose that is especially true when you've been married—shall we say 'several' times?"

"May I ask you a personal question?" I smiled ingratiatingly.

"If you get me another one of these," she said lifting her empty glass. I did.

"Ask away."

"Are you ever afraid that Reginald will, well, hurt

you in some way?"

Suddenly I felt cold hands tighten around my throat.

That familiar man's voice spoke behind me. "She's not afraid, but you better be."

I felt my eyes bulging, ready to pop from my forehead like two marbles in the barrels of a double-barreled shot gun. Then little squiggly worms swam in the blackness.

Then they stopped swimming.

11

Ice-cold water slapped my face, and so did a pair of ice-cold hands. When I finally cracked my eyes open, they were staring up at a panicked and contrite face. "Oh, God, Gil, am I glad you're okay. My God, I was joking; I had no idea you'd pass out like that. Are you okay, pal?"

I just looked at him. My face must have had a foreboding blankness to it. My voice didn't seem to be anywhere in the vicinity.

"Gil, baby, tell me you're all right!"

I didn't. I noticed Harriet was behind him, and she was giving him the Lucifer for putting me under like that. But I still couldn't utter a sound. I may have been all right, but the room definitely wasn't—it was turning upside down and back again.

"Geez, Honeycakes, you think I choked his voice box closed or something?"

"Maybe we should take him to the doctor."

"Geez—they'll put me off the ship. Jail maybe. Gil, baby," he was slapping my cheeks again and it was getting annoying. *Speak* to me. *Say* something." But I just stared. That was the other thing: I didn't seem to be able to close my eyes.

Carting him off to jail, I had to admit, was a delightful prospect. My problem solved, my fee earned. Then I heard Harriet's voice:

"He wouldn't do that, Reginald. He wouldn't take

you from me," she said. "But I think we have to get him to the doctor. There could be something seriously wrong with him."

"He'll be okay," I heard the voice coming from somewhere. They were both standing over me and the voice, disembodied as it was, must have been Reginald's. I only wished he sounded more concerned. *I* was concerned, but I couldn't say so.

"Do you want to go to the doc, pal?" Reg asked. I was beginning to wonder about his intellect. He saw I couldn't talk and yet asked me this crucial question. I suppose so he could say he asked if I wanted to go, and I didn't say I did.

I opened my mouth to shout "yes" but nothing came out. I tried to nod my head, but it wouldn't nod. For my part, I wished I'd negotiated a medical plan out of old Harvey Soft Tobacco Cakes. I don't have to tell you Daddybucks, my employer, was miles too cheap to have one for his minions.

"I think we should take him," Harriet said.

"Why don't we wait a couple of minutes? He'll snap out of it. He was just scared."

'Well, I don't *blame* him," she said. "I'm scared myself."

"I was only joking. How was I to know he'd freak out? I just surprised him, I guess. What were you talking about anyway?"

"Nothing..."

"Come on Gil," he tapped me lightly on the jaw with his fist, like he was my best buddy. I didn't think I should lose my sense of humor, just because I lost my speech. Why couldn't Tyranny Rex, my beloved wife, be the one to lose her sense of speech?

"Maybe he's had a stroke!" Harriet said. She seemed to be the only one with real concern. "Come on, Reg, we can't wait any longer. I'm calling the doctor."

"Wait a minute," he said, putting out his hand to restrain her, though she hadn't yet made a move. "How is this going to look? I think first we have to agree I just touched him from behind while he was talking to you, and he blacked out—had his stroke or whatever."

"Well..."

"Maybe with my horsing around I snapped something in his neck that knocked out his speech. What then?"

"Well, Reg, you didn't do it on *purpose*."

"No, no, I didn't. No. So we'll have to be sure we tell that the same. I could be in a lot of trouble. Geez, what a stupid thing to do. But I hardly touched him! He must be one sensitive guy. I guess I just scared the hell out of him."

And that was the story they told to the doctor. He was a short, portly guy who specialized in facial hair. It was black and white and bushy-bristly. He had a deep voice that reminded me of Old Beefy. But his facial features were more regular-guy clean.

He gave me the flashlight in the eye treatment, the stethoscope to the heart, the blood pressure grabber. If he had any ideas he kept them to himself.

This seemed to agitate Reginald. "So what's up, Doc?" he asked, fidgeting. We were in the bowels of the ship—the low-rent district to us penthousers, and the space devoted to the healing arts was not immodest. They probably figured the doc was considered godlike enough without installing him in a cathedral.

If I could have spoken, I would have directed the doctor's attention to my neck. There must have been marks there the way Reg had choked me. But again, no one said "boo" about them, if they were indeed there.

But the doctor didn't commit himself. "I think we'd better keep him here for observation."

"What are you going to observe?"

"Heart rate, blood pressure, any unusual vital signs," the doctor said. "You have any objections?"

"No, I...I guess I don't know, do we have some sort of responsibility here?"

"I don't know, do you?"

"For his bill, I mean. Obviously he's not in any shape

to sign himself in, and we hardly know him."

The doctor raised a hand to cut off debate. "Don't worry about that," he said. "But let me understand what happened again."

"I told you," Reginald said, expressing some exasperation. "He was talking in the Oak Room to Harriet here. I was in the casino. I came up from behind and put my arms on his shoulders and he seemed to go rigid, then he tipped over. In no time he opened his eyes. I said I was sorry I scared him, and was he all right and all, but we couldn't get him to talk after that."

"Could he have had a stroke?" Harriet asked.

"Could have," the doctor said, stroking the forest on his face. "Well, thank you for calling me. I'll see he gets the best we have to offer. Where can I find you if I need you?"

"We're in Penthouse seventeen—Harriet Himmelfarb and Reginald Windsor."

I may have imagined it, but I thought I detected a flicker of doubt in the doctor's eyebrows. He thanked them again, shooed them out the door, closed it politely but firmly, then came back to where I was reclining on the examining table.

"Okay, Mr. Yates," he said, "to paraphrase Mr. Reginald Windsor, 'What's up?'"

And that was it. As soon as I saw their backs pouring out the door, I found my voice. "I don't know," I said. "That man tried to choke me. I guess I panicked."

"Any idea why he tried to choke you?"

There it was, on the table. I quickly realized I didn't want to blow my cover. Casting suspicions on Reg might work for or against me. I didn't want Harriet throwing herself at him in some sympathy reaction.

"I think he got irrationally jealous of me talking to his woman friend," I said. "God, that's the most improbable thing. She's about twice my age."

"I daresay," the doctor said. "Well, I thought this might have been a ruse. I couldn't find any indication you'd had that magnitude of a trauma. A young healthy man like you shouldn't be scared speechless by the mere surprise of someone behind you. And as I say, I didn't see anything—except maybe where he '*touched* you on the shoulder,' and left these lovely black and blue marks on your neck. You want me to lock him up for the rest of the cruise, or do you think you can stay away from him?"

"I think I'll be okay," I said. "But, I will be more careful. Maybe I'll have dinner in my room just to keep him worried that he's done some permanent damage."

The doctor released me with a handshake, and I hurried to my cabin to hear what Harriet and Reginald had to say about the little caper.

12

It was thus that came about a subtle but critical change in the dynamics of my assignment. Now I was not only charged with keeping Harriet Himmelfarb alive and well, and intact with her money, I had to keep myself alive as well. As for my handsome fee, if I wasn't alive, I couldn't collect.

My obvious, safest course was to forget the whole thing, keep my distance from the lucky couple and preserve my being. My paranoia was whispering to me that what with Reg's background and all, he could well have discovered the bug, and somehow found out I was on the other end of it. That friendly choking would certainly lend itself to that hypothesis.

In my favor, we established that I had been attacked by this genial con man. Soon I must let him know, as subtly as possible, that I knew what happened, and so did the doctor and his nurse. So it wouldn't be wise to try it again.

But murderers are, alas, not always the souls of logic. So I had to decide, was it worth risking my life to preserve Harvey Cavendish's inheritance? Even if he sent my hundred-and-fifty-grand fee to my widow? That would be, for Tyranny's father the pernurious Daddybucks, a drop in the spittoon.

I knew I had to decide, and I decided to put off my decision. For verily it is said, why do today what you can think about tomorrow.

The next morning I had breakfast in my penthouse—out on the veranda, it was so balmy. We were getting closer to the equator and November was warming up.

The clouds looked like rows of pure white cotton candy that had been nibbled at. They sat on the edge of the ocean poised to recycle their water. It was paradise for an old city boy like myself. I just ruminated on my chances. All I had to do to earn my $150,000 was bring her back alive and unmarried, or alive and married with a prenuptial contract.

When I finished breakfast, my phone rang. Without thinking, I picked it up.

"Gil my boy, good to hear your voice. It's Reg. Listen Gil, I've got to talk to you. This has been a terrible trauma for me too. I haven't been able to sleep. Let's get together and thrash this thing out. I feel so *terrible* about it, honestly I do. I've got to convince you I didn't mean anything. What do you say?"

What I said was nothing. It didn't take a genius to tell I was being conned. He didn't have the slightest trouble sleeping. I had a tape full of his snoring.

"Gil, are you there?"

"Reg, I'm sorry, I just don't feel up to your company at the moment."

"Gil! You *do* have hard feelings."

"That's on the bucks, Reg."

"On the bucks? What's that mean? Oh, you mean on the money."

"Whatever."

"Let's talk about it. What can it hurt?"

"The last time it hurt a lot, believe me," I said. "Sorry, but I'm going to keep my back to the wall for the rest of the trip and I plan to give you a wide swatch."

"Swath? A wide swath."

"Whatever," I said as I hung up.

Just to give myself more breathing room, I had lunch on deck. A nice, juicy hamburger with the works. I had no trouble avoiding the constant couple. They took all their meals in the dining room, and I expect Reginald had hopes of my showing up.

Dinner, I decided, should be my re-entry. I timed it to arrive early in the hope that the Princess Romanoff would be there to protect me.

She was, and when I began the conversation with some inane pleasantry she almost fell into a swoon.

By the time Reginald and Harriet came to the table, I had insulated myself with the princess on one side of me and Chesty and his frau on the other.

"Whew, it's sure good to see you up and about," Reginald said, as he sat down next to Lillith. "He gave us quite a start," he announced to the table. "I told you he passed out while we were talking to him—we rushed him to the hospital and we were on tether hooks, but I'm tickled pink to see him, well in the *pink!*" he beamed his happiness across our universe.

The waiter appeared with the menus and did his bow tie trick—He would bob his Adam's apple up and down and the black bow tie went with it. He was becoming famous for it. So famous, if he didn't do it Chesty would boom "Dance the bow tie, Whore Hey!" So rather than hear the "whore" pronunciation of his name, he danced it virtually every time you looked at him.

Maine lobster was on the menu. We all ordered it except Old Beefy who said, "Steak and fries. Rare! And bring catsup and A.1. sauce."

"Feeling all right are you, Gil?" Reginald wouldn't leave it alone. I just stared at him. "I mean you're looking good, so I assume everything turned out all right."

Chesty came to my rescue. "Never assume *any-thing,*" he said in that table-ware-rattling voice of his. It makes an *ass* out of *u* and *me,*" he smiled, and to see Chesty smile you had to look closely because there was very little movement in those thin, anemic lips. "So what happened to you, Gil?" he asked. Now I was on the spot. I had been willing to not argue with Reginald's gratuitous version, but now that I was asked point *blanche,* I thought the best part of valor would be to get my story on record. It might make Reginald think twice if he took it in his head to try to take me out of the picture subsequently.

"It was the strangest thing." I began, eyeing Reginald to see if he squirmed. My beginning was innocuous enough. I wanted to keep it that way. "I was in the Oak Room talking to Harriet. My back was to the casino, when suddenly I felt these hands around my neck, tightening, and that's the last I remember."

"You choked him?" Chesty asked Reginald like he was shooting a bazooka at him.

"No, I put my hands on his shoulders. I guess I did it so suddenly, he fainted. There wasn't any choking involved—" he paused and turned to his girlfriend. "Was there, Harriet?"

She didn't answer right away, and for a moment I thought she was going to make a clean bosom of it. Then she said in a quiet, noncommittal voice, "I didn't see any."

Reginald was beginning to perspire. "You know, I guess I am just a strong guy," he said, mopping his brow with his handkerchief. "I used to play four sets of tennis a day, no sweat. I underestimate my strength sometimes, I guess."

"That choking's a bad business," Chesty said. "I was in the Navy at boot camp when a guy died from one of those horsing around chokings. Never mess with somebody's neck. Very sensitive. They put the guy who did it away for a couple years for manslaughter. I say they should have shot him. Anything else—too good." Chesty's opinions had a way of sounding like universal truths.

Reginald frowned and droplets of stress sweat showed on his bald forehead. "Well, it was an accident," he said, "and I won't put my hands anywhere near anyone's shoulders again."

"Not even mine?" the sex kitten next to him asked coyly, her eyelashes doing the tango.

Lillith was the sensitive one at the table. How she could be otherwise and be married to that opinionated heap of digested beef was everybody's guess. In her squeaky, small voice she asked Harriet, "Are you making any progress towards your wedding?"

"I'm still thinking," Harriet said giving *her* eyelashes a workout. This girlish display from a seventy-six year old baffled me. Did people act like teenagers all their lives? Perhaps I was out of touch, being one of the youngest passengers by far on this cruise. I did find it interesting that the staff, the keepers of this zoo, were all very young. Was it to make the old fogies feel young again? Would it be just *too* depressing to be surrounded by people from the same geriatric reaches of time? Of course, if the staff and crew were that old, they could hardly function.

"Still thinking?" Chesty sounded off for the entire dining room. "What are you thinking about?"

"Oh, lots of things," Harriet said smugly.

"Are you thinking about having his hands tightening on your neck? Just for a joke?"

I was thrilled with that from Old Beefy, but loving-Harriet came through, "Oh no, I'm not afraid of Reginald. He's the kindest, gentlest man I've ever known."

A sound like, "Harumph" came from Chesty.

"Day after tomorrow is Tahiti," Lillith said, as though the conversation had never left her track. "And the next day is Moorea. In Moorea they have this wedding store, and traditionally people get married there. Chester and I were talking and we were saying that might be a nice place to get married."

"I thought you *were* married," Harriet said.

"Yes, we are, but *you*.... I hope you'll invite us all if you *do*. I love weddings."

"Me too." The princess was offering her input.

"Sounds good to me," Reginald said. "How about you, Hon?"

"I thought you wanted the captain to do the ceremony. Aboard the ship."

"Sure, if you'd rather. You decide."

I am so sorry to say she looked like she *was* thinking.

13

At dinner the night before Tahiti, the princess stunned me speechless.

"I'm so looking forward to tomorrow," she said. "I'm taking a car to the botanic garden on the other side of the island. They have *beaucoup* palm trees, and I just adore palms. They grow here like weeds."

"All look alike to me," Chesty said, chewing a mouthful of steak, rare.

"Oh, but Tahiti has palms we can't grow in the States," she enthused. "*Pritchardia vuylstekeana, Pelagodoxa henryana, Cocos nucifera*, all kinds of yummies."

I felt my jaw rattle the china on the table when she turned to me. "Do you like palms, Gil?"

I don't know how long it took for words to pass over my slack jaw. When I finally heard the sounds, they said something like, "Well...I...yes...I...ah, do. I have a number of...ah, palms in my garden."

"Good," she clapped her hands together once. "Do you want to ride along?" she said. "I'll pay, of course—my late husband left me rather well off..."

"Oh, ah, well," I stammered. "Perhaps someone else would like to, too. We could make a party of it. Reginald?"

"Nah," he said. "I don't do trees."

"Harriet?" I asked.

"I'm feeling a little under the weather at the moment. Maybe tomorrow I'll just rest in our penthouse."

She seemed to delight in pronouncing *penthouse* when she could have underplayed it by saying cabin.

"Well, if you aren't going ashore, doll," Reginald said. "Perhaps, I should stay by your side."

"Don't be silly, love. You want to see the sights."

"Well—if you think it's okay—I *would* like to go ashore."

"Want to join us Chester—Lillith?" I asked.

"Oh, thank you," Lillith said, "but we're going to do the shops."

"Can't keep her out of the shops," Chesty boomed, then laughed a hearty, chesty laugh as though he had just said the funniest thing he had ever heard.

"Reginald, come with us to see the palms," I said.

"Palms? Seriously? Palm trees? You're going across the island to see palms? I got news for you. You can see them from the ship, pal."

"Ah, but you see one or two types in Papeete—at the botanic garden you'll see hundreds," I said.

"And they'll all look alike."

"No they won't," Sophia chimed in. "I'll show you the differences."

"Yes," Harriet said, "Why not? I'm going to be resting, you want to get off the ship, don't you?"

"Nah, I'll stay with you, babe."

I went rigid inside. Good as Sophia was beginning to look, I was afraid to leave Harriet alone with Reginald.

"Oh, come on, Reginald," Sophia said, "don't be such a party pooper."

"Oh, well, geezus, why not?" he said, then turned to Harriet. "You sure it's all right, babe?"

"Oh, yes," she said, as if exasperated with his recalcitrance. "Go! I want you to."

He looked at me and shrugged. "Okay, pal," he said, "you win."

I must have let out enough air to float a 747.

So the deal was made.

I couldn't believe the princess liked palms. I would

have suspected her of reading up to make a play for me, but I had told no one of my interest. I realized our maid put my palm pictures up on the mirror in my cabin (penthouse to Harriet). But surely Sophia's maid was a different person. Could they have been roommates? More food for paranoia. Besides, how could she have known those Latin names?

We made Tahiti at dawn the next morning. It felt good to feel the huge ship bang against the dock, signaling our first land in more than a week.

The island of Tahiti is a nice-looking place from the ocean. But something has happened to it. It now has an ersatz commercial center, and it seems to me to be the wrong place for a thriving metropolis: stores that purvey leather goods and perfumes (one gardenia used to do the job here, I'm told), hamburgers and designer jeans.

Islands in the South Pacific conjure up visions of half-naked natives lolling knee deep in an azure briny ocean, eating breadfruit, mangoes and coconut as they fall from the trees. No automobiles, no telephones. Just gorgeous primitives whose features have been refined by centuries of crossbreeding as well as a dollop of inbreeding. They are the people who gave birth to our expression, "laid back." They haven't a care in the world, and when they feel like mating they do. With anybody, anytime, anywhere.

That's the vision, but, as I said, something has been rotten in the woodpile.

The emissaries of a mysterious and distant religion have cinched up the girls in brassieres and pretty-much ruined the place. It is no small irony that if you want to see girls unruined by breast guards, you have to go west to the source of the missionaries.

Physician, heal thy own ball of wax.

Heretofore, when a guy died here, the women would flagellate themselves, collect the blood on cloth, sun-dry it and present it to his survivors as a token of their high regard. Now *there's* a heart-rending custom. The western religious mood-shapers frown on the practice as "barbaric". Pity.

I met Sophia, my princess-for-a-day at the door for

disembarking. She had on a brightly colored sarong that she must have imagined made her look like a native. On her head she had a broad-brimmed straw hat that fell short of covering all that faux-flaxen hair. She was gussied up to kill, but I was going with her for insurance *against* being killed.

"Oh, Gil, how nice to see you," she greeted me with an infusion of effusion. "Can you believe it, I thought you might not come, might be playing me along or something, but here you are and I'm as ready as I can be. We're going to have a wonderful day, don't you think? Well, I do. It's going to be *splendid!* Oh, Gil, I've been so looking forward to it. It's not easy being a woman alone on one of these things, believe me, you're like an outcast, an anathema, and don't I know it. Just look around, how many men do you see? It must be twenty-to-one on here—women to men, have you noticed?"

"No, I—"

"So I just think I'm the luckiest woman alive to have an *escort* to Papeete, Tahiti, and the botanic garden. Shall we go?" she asked, taking my arm.

"Well, yes, but aren't we waiting for Reginald?"

"Oh," she said, putting her long fingers to her lips, "I *completely* forgot."

Fortunately, Reginald hadn't forgotten and he came bounding up.

"Palm trees," he said, shaking his head. "I must be nuts."

The smashing young ship's photographer, in white Bermuda shorts and a sheer navy top hustled us at the bottom of the gangplank to take our picture. I tried to nix it but the princess said, "Oh, let's." And we did.

At the dock, there stood a crane reaching to the sky almost as high as the ship. Dangling from the cable high up on the crane was a platform with a three-sided fence around it. From the fourth and front side, a young woman girded at both ankles with elastic belts took a dive into the sky and fell to the earth. She was caught short by the straps and bounced up and down like a yo-yo.

"Bungee jumping," Sophia exclaimed, clapping her hands. "Let's do it! It would be such fun, hey Gil? Come on, what do you say?"

"No thanks."

"Reginald?"

"Don't look at me," he said.

"I'll pay," she said, looking at me again.

"In advance, I'm sure," I said.

"Oh come on, Gil, it's not dangerous. Look, even if something happened to *one* of the straps, there are two of them."

"Fine, you go," I said. "Reg and I'll go to the botanic garden."

"Oh, you're such a stick-in-the-mud."

"But my head is up," I said. "I went on that thing I'd be stuck in the mud head down."

She pouted for only a short while, and we went to the car she had arranged through the ship's shore travel office to have waiting for us at the dock. She signed some papers with the attendant and we piled in, Reginald gallantly taking the back, and I turning to keep my eyes on him. He was, I thought, situated a little too conveniently for strangling me from behind.

The commercial core of this island paradise was close to the dock. As with most of these idyllic South Sea islands, a road hugged the circumference of the place and the middle was a hump of desolate land, in some venues housing a volcano or two.

As we approached the core, Sophia bore the burden of the small-talk: "Isn't it a lovely day?" ("Oh, yes.")—"Isn't the weather pleasant?" ("It is.")—"Isn't this a nice little car?" (emphasis on little).

I realized this mindless chatter should have been annoying me, and in most circumstances, it would have. But her voice, verging on the squeaky, had an engaging lilt to it—as if mindless babble were sung set to music.

There comes a time when female companionship for the male takes precedence over life itself. I was beginning to feel an encroaching precedence. And she knew *palms!*

We couldn't have gone more than three blocks when I was sorry Reginald was in the backseat providing us with an unwanted chaperone. You know what they say, "Two's company, but with three you get eggroll."

Looking at him, I could tell he was not as enchanted with Sophia's ramblings as I was. Obviously he had bigger fillies to fry. He looked like a man who was about to jump out of the car. Then at the next stoplight, he did.

En route I heard him say, "Sorry, pal, I don't think palm trees are my cup of tea. I'm gonna check out the local saloons—get the flavor of the place—toodle-oo." And he was gone and I'm ashamed to say, I was glad.

"Phew," Sophia said. "I thought he'd never leave," and we both had a good laugh.

We drove in silence, each eyeing the other at shortening intervals; taking in the outside scenery at first, then gradually concentrating more on the interior.

"You know, Gil," Sophia said, smiling at me. "You don't scare me. I like that."

I gulped.

"Guys built like Schwarzenegger scare me. I don't want to be scared any more."

"You used to be scared, Sophia?"

She nodded, closing her eyes to shut out some past horror.

"Of what?" I asked.

"Oh," she said, waving a hand as if to pass it off, "I had an addiction. Almost destroyed me."

"But it didn't," I said, being careful not to make it sound like an astonished question.

"Well, I lost two husbands and almost a third. But, God bless him, he saved me."

"So, you're still married?" I asked, and for some reason, I hoped she wasn't.

"No," she said, with a catch in her voice. "He's gone."

"Oh, I'm sorry," I said.

"But I'll never forget him. He was my salvation—my everything." She sucked in her lips. "My addiction was to games of chance. It became all-consuming. It not only cost me my first two husbands—I broke them both in the process. I could not shake this obsession. It was not about getting rich; it was the thrill of the chase. Deep down I knew if I won big I'd only try to win bigger and fail in the process. But I couldn't help myself."

"But you're third husband got you out of it?"

"Yes." Her eyes got a faraway look, as if she were grasping to relive the happiness.

"How did he do it?" I said. "I expect *you* ultimately had to do it yourself."

"Well, ultimately, perhaps—but he gave me love and encouragement and understanding—commodities hard to come by in this day and age, believe you me. He lived for me," she said, nostalgia thick in her voice.

And died for you, I added the missing words, but not outloud. "He must have been some guy."

"That he was," she sighed. "It's thanks to him I'm on this cruise."

Sitting there in the car with Sophia, I was feeling a familiar warmth as in when the opposites of the species come in close proximity. If anyone could make me forget Reginald and Harriet, it was she.

It's funny how people you aren't sure about start to look better and better when there's no one else you're sure about. It was the alone-on-a-desert-island syndrome.

Here we were, alone on a tropical island and punch couldn't have been any more pleased than I was.

From the air above, Tahiti was an island shaped like an "8"—and it was broader at the bottom, like a lot of people.

The ship had docked at the bottom of the bottom of the "8", at the metropolis of Papeete. The Harrison W. Smith Botanical Gardens, 340 acres in all, was in Papeari, at the top of the bottom of the "8", so to speak. It was next to the Gauguin Museum. We hit that first. Gauguin may have been the most glamorous of the impressionists, dumping his wife like he did to sail for Tahiti, B.B. (before brassiers) in his pursuit of his art and the nubile natives.

I can relate.

As soon as Sophia and I left the car to begin our stroll in the botanic garden, she reached for my hand. I surrendered it. She had long, bony fingers and warm, smooth skin. It was an apt introduction to paradise. For this *was* truly a palm-lovers paradise. I mean, they were all over the place—a forest of palms almost. I had never seen anything like it for rare and unusual species. The closest thing we had in Southern California was the Huntington palm garden in Pasadena, and they couldn't grow all this stuff there. Here, everything looked good. And *tall*, too. In my garden, I'd planted a lot of different palms and cycads, but they were pipsqueaks still—coming up to my knees, a couple to my chest. Here were a couple of *Cycas circinalis* that towered over me. Surely they'd take over a hundred years to get that tall where I came from.

Everything was lush and green thanks to nature's watering system. They even had grass here, though they didn't seem fastidious about its care. Mowing was about it, and that sporadically.

"Look," Sophia said, "a *Brahea clara*. I've never seen one of those."

"I haven't either—"

"Look," she exclaimed like a child in a candy store, "coconuts everywhere."

"*Cocos nucifera*," I said, showing off about the most common palm in the South Seas—one we couldn't grow at all.

Every time we saw an exciting palm, Sophia squeezed my hand. I thought I was going to be black and blue before long.

Walking under all these tall palms was exhilarating, or was it because of the proximity—and timing—of Sophia?

"Oh, look, here's the *Pritchardia vuylstekeana*," she said. "Aren't those leaves gorgeous?"

I admitted they were. She squeezed my hand and said, "So are you," then gave me a kiss on the cheek.

There were only a few visitors to the garden, no one, as far as I could see, from the ship. They were all in the shops and saloons. I only hoped Reginald was comfy on a bar stool somewhere and wasn't back in his penthouse wreaking havoc on Harriet.

We were stopped in a private grove of palms by an expanse of water, and a cursory glance about told us we were alone. Sophia quickly turned my thought from impending disaster shipside to a pleasant disaster of my own. She moved her lips in one undaunting motion from my check to my lips.

I gotta say this for Sophia, she knew how to kiss—that's no kidding around. In the right circumstances, one torrid kiss from her would melt a whole carload of glass figurines. And for some reason, *this* seemed to be the right circumstances.

Somehow, I found myself leaning against the fat trunk of a *Jubaea chilensis*, the Chilean wine palm which is massacred in its native habitat for the yummy you-know-what.

Princess Sophia Romanoff was pressing against me and I was feeling things I hadn't felt in some time. She was not a shy woman. You might even say she was aggressive to a fault, and I, being the aforementioned pushover, was powerless to resist. Even though we had a good eight more hours before sailing, I had a foreboding that we might miss the boat.

I feel that here I should exercise my right of privacy that one of the Supremes made up awhile back. Suffice it to say that there against the fat trunk of that *Jubaea chilensis*, Princess Romanoff made me feel very presidential.

On the drive back to Papeete we held hands, communicating with euphoric silence.

The reality of the city broke the spell as soon as we parked the car.

Strolling through the commercial center of this incongruous metropolis made me wonder what annoyed me more, the surfeit of knickknack shops or the brassieres. Both were big disappointments.

For here, in what, heretofore, was noted for sand and compliant women, was Miami Beach without the zoning ordinances. Women who used to laze around on the beach sans underwear, sucking on coconuts, now dressed like librarians in Wichita, Kansas, and hustled TV sets.

"Where do we return the car?" I asked.

"Down the main drag," she said. "Don't you want to see the shops?"

"No." I said resoundingly. I was, as they say in the vernacular, shotsky.

We saw the shops anyway.

Between four-story buildings, we found shops that specialized in leather goods, electronic equipment and superfluous objects made from coconuts. It put me in mind of the products of a certain glass blower of my acquaintance. "Art is in the eye of the beholder," Sophia said, when I complained about the uselessness of it all.

We passed a place that reminded me of a Las Vegas wedding chapel. "Oh, look, Gil," she said. "What a cute place for Reginald and Prune to get married."

"Oh, geez," I said. "You think they will?"

"She'd be nuts not to," she said.

"You think so?"

"You bet. A woman like that—almost eighty years old, so many facelifts Seinfeld couldn't make her smile. My God, where is she going to find a man? I don't care *how* rich she is. She's playing so coy I'm getting a stomachache from listening to her reluctance. If he weren't asking her, she'd be begging him."

We were in front of a two-story marketplace, Tahiti's

answer to the shopping mall, when Sophia said, "I'm going to pop in here and go to the little girls' room. You *will* wait here for me, won't you?"

I said I would and she was gone. I passed the time looking at the produce in the marketplace into which Sophia had disappeared. The fruits and vegetables seemed to have been pretty much picked over, like we had arrived on the cusp of closing time. The remaining dead fish, strung up on wooden stakes, seemed lonely.

I wandered back out onto the street where Sophia had left me, like the loyal lap dog I had become after twenty-some years of marriage to Dorcas Wemple, my Tyranny Rex.

I hadn't seen it coming. It was a rock the size of a basketball and it must have just fallen out of the second story of the market. It hit me on the shoulder and tore down my chest and right arm, slicing me like a hunk of salami. Then it rolled to rest in the street against an automobile tire. I know because I was lying right there next to it.

It was a strange-looking rock. It was full of holes and brownish, and as I lay there dazed and staring at it I could have sworn I saw Reginald Windsor's face in it.

There I was at tire level, cars running by me as though nothing had happened. No one even slowed down to roll down a window and ask if I was all right. Miami Beach for sure.

I saw my reflection in the shiny hubcap of a parked car. In my delirium I visualized myself on a round television screen. It was like I was the bloody victim in one of those bang-bang cop shows.

The slices on my body were pouring my precious blood onto the streets of Papeete. Of course my cuts smarted a bit, but my mind was on the struggle to remain conscious.

I failed.

14

When I awoke my sense of time was out of joint, so I don't know how long I was lying in the street of the sun-drenched sand paradise.

"Gil—oh my God, Gil!" was the shrieking that returned me to consciousness. It was the Russian princess. "What happened? Gil, are you all right—? Oh, my God. Gil! Gil?"

I think I groaned, but my memory was out to breakfast and it was lunchtime.

"What happened, Gil?"

"Rock," I said. "I dunno..." I wasn't in shape to be too articulate.

Sophia insisted I see the doctor. I said I wasn't really hurt, just stunned and a little scraping of skin—

"A little!" she shouted. "There's blood all over you."

"It won't matter," I said. "Harriet will swear that Reginald was with her when it happened. Maybe he was. Maybe he paid somebody."

"Pooh!" she said. "You're paranoid."

"Besides calling attention to all this may make him more eager to put me away," I said, grogilly. "We might be better off making believe nothing happened."

"All right. See the doctor, *then* make believe."

She was persuasive, and that's what I did. I don't remember how she got me back to the ship. I guess she still had the rental car.

The doctor was a good sport. "You again," he said. I protested that I didn't want to bother him, but Sophia insisted.

"You must be some kind of hypochondriac to come to a doctor for this superficial 'stuff'," I saw him wink at Sophia—I'm sure he wanted me to see it. "First you imagine a guy almost choking you to death, now you imagine all these bloody abrasions. Too bad we don't have a psychiatrist aboard."

The doctor patched me up; some antiseptic and bandages which I covered with a long-sleeved shirt. "This will be confidential?" I asked. "I'm not eager to aggravate anyone into repeating this stuff."

"You know what Hippocrates said," he offered.

"No, I..."

"It doesn't matter, he was a hypocrite anyway."

That seemed to me short of a commitment, and such was the state of my overripe paranoia that I wondered if the doctor was in on it.

Sophia wanted to nurse me in her cabin, and I didn't want her to know where mine was. I was frankly panicked to get back to my listening post to tune in on Reginald and Harriet. I was sure he had done this to me so he could fix Harriet for good without my meddling. I finally convinced her I was all right, but as soon as I got into my digs I collapsed on the bed.

There were sounds coming from the next cabin. Tuning in to the tape, I came in in the middle of something.

"You're the only one I have eyes for," Harriet was saying. "You're my sweetheart."

"You mean that, doll?"

"Of course I mean that."

"Then let's do it!"

There was a silence during which I imagined him taking her in his arms and kissing her.

"Oh Reg," she swooned at last. "You certainly are persistent."

"Good!" he said. "That's what I want to be. You're

worth it. It isn't right that a wonderful woman like you should be without a husband while so many inferior girls strut their stuff with a husband in tow. It just isn't right."

"What about the agreement?" She asked in her little girl, you-are-overcoming-me-with-your-macho-persuasion voice.

"I'm sure the ship will give us the license."

"Reginald," she said, "I'm talking about the prenuptial agreement."

"Oh, yes, right. Sure. Let's make it up right now. What do you want it to say?"

Another pause. "I'm not sure."

"So shall we wait until you know? I'm no lawyer, but I think with your will intact it won't matter that you married." Again the silence. He was accomplished at the pregnant pause.

"But I don't have a will," she said.

"You what?" Our actor sounded shocked. "No will—? Then maybe you should just make a will first, leaving everything to Harvey."

"I don't want to leave everything to Harvey," Harriet said.

"Of course—stupid me—you have a daughter."

"She doesn't need it."

"Well, Jesus, Harriet, you've got to have a will. Harvey is counting on that money. You don't want to disappoint him."

"Oh, I don't know," she said. "What I don't want to do is die."

"Of course not, Honeycakes. But we all die and it doesn't hurt to be prepared," Reginald said. "You want to do something for your loved ones at the end."

Oh my God, I thought, I am listening to the operation of a master. As smooth as fine polyester, and she is drinking it down, hood, line and clinker.

"I'm afraid Harvey has been leery of all my husbands. He's suspected each one was after me for my money."

"Were they?"

"How can you know? I suppose everybody is mercenary."

"I'm not," he said. "And I want to prove it. Let's make a will right now."

"Now? Don't you need a lawyer for that?"

"Not really. We'll make a simple will, all you have to do is say you are of sound mind, sign it and date it. You can say anything you want and it will be legal."

"That part about the sound mind. You think I am of sound mind, don't you?"

"Of course. How can you ask such a thing?"

"And you want to marry me?"

"Yes."

"Even if you don't get a farthing?"

"Absolutely—"

"Then how could I refuse you," she said. "I accept!"

There were the beautiful sounds of love, turned sour in my ears as my eyes saw my fee starting to sprout wings. Didn't Harriet know about dying intestate—without a will—and the spouse taking the whole pot?

I was the first one at the table that night for dinner. Sophia was next and she eased into the chair next to me, and before I knew it I felt a stockinged foot caressing my ankle.

"Gil!" she exclaimed, "How *are* you?"

"I'm fine," I said, but I don't think she believed me.

Unfortunately the next couple to the table was the engaged pair. Of course, I couldn't let on that I knew about the engagement.

Reginald put his hands gently on my shoulder, announcing to the world what a lamb he was. Then he quickly withdrew them and said, "Whoops, sorry, I forgot. Can't scare you. You okay, Gil? Still doing okay?" His face was sagging as though part of a timed meltdown. He didn't look as happy as I thought a man who just got engaged should.

"Still alive," I said, with a sardonic sneer.

He sat down right next to me. Naturally.

"Hey Horehay," he summoned our short, bow-tied

waiter—who came to us, bobbing his bow tie. "Where's the wine guy? We want some champagne to start the celebration." Reginald was always a demonstrable, happy guy, but now he was happy-go-lucky. Except for his face. It was troubled.

The wine steward appeared, a slight chap with a pencil moustache, wire-rimmed James Joyce glasses and one of those ridiculous silver cups on a chain around his neck. He wore a maroon jacket which set him off from a mere waiter who wore only a maroon vest.

Chesty and Lillith sat as Reginald was grilling the wine steward. "We'd like to start off with something special tonight, for a special occasion."

"Were you thinking perhaps of champagne, sir?"

"I was, yes," Reginald said. "To start."

"The Dom Pérignon, *Moët et Chandon* is very nice, sir."

"Let's have it," Reginald said.

"Champagne," Beefy boomed. "That stuff's a hundred and five bucks a bottle!"

"Only live once, Chester," Reginald said, trying to match the boom of Beefy and falling short. "This is a *big* night for us and we want you all to share in it." Reginald left it at that but no one was in much doubt. He wasn't buying a hundred and five dollar bottle of champagne to celebrate my near miss in Papeete.

Then the maroon-jacketed, pencil-moustached chap with the James Joyce glasses returned carrying the bottle like it was a precious child. He plopped it into the silver bucket that reposed tableside for just such eventualities. Then with a napkin, a corkscrew and a flourish of elbows and wrists he decorked the vessel and poured a glass for Harriet and another for the host.

"All around, Jeeves," Reginald said, accenting his faux Britishness. "Give 'em all a glass." And Jeeves, whose nameplate called him Franco, obliged.

When all the glasses were filled, Franco bowed and retreated, depositing the bottle back in its silver bucket.

Then with a deep relish that suffused his big body and cast the glow of health and happiness across him like a Christmas blanket, Reginald Windsor lifted his glass and crowed, "I have a toast to make." He checked us all to see that we picked up our glasses. When this was accomplished, he cleared his throat and began:

"Here's to the most wonderful woman in the world. A woman who has given me untold happiness with her charm, her wit and her intelligence."

And money, I added to myself.

"A woman whom any man would be lucky to have as his wife—a woman who has made me the luckiest man in the world by so graciously accepting my humble proposal of marriage. To my perfect bride-to-be, my beloved, my life, my love, Harriet Himmelfarb."

Lillith cooed, Beefy grunted, Sophia gasped, and I blended in with an "ah," just to make the whole thing seem a happy, festive occasion.

Chesty said, "So, he finally wore you down!"

Harriet cooed in harmony with Lillith and allowed as how she was a very lucky woman herself. Her face showed her pride at landing a substantially younger man. Reginald "Bluebeard" Windsor's face still troubled me. For while he was making all the appropriate sounds and gestures, he looked like a man whose mind was not on heavenly things.

It was beef Wellington for dinner, all around.

Beefy said, "Rare! And bring the A.1. Sauce."

I ate reluctantly, because all that ground-up goose liver they put between the crust and the meat makes me gag. It's a mystery to me how anyone can find that tasty.

To accompany the dinner, Reginald, with Harriet's expressed approval, ordered a bottle of Château Lafite-Rothschild—first growth, whatever that means. It was a $155 the pop.

Chesty and I didn't drink, and Lillith took only a few sociable sips and exclaimed in her high-pitched, girly voice, "It is simply delightful!"

With the news, Sophia had abruptly ceased massaging my ankle with her foot. I looked over at her and she seemed sad and reflective. She hadn't touched her wine. It sat in her glass shimmering from the lights, yet looking somewhat forlorn just as she did.

"Something wrong?" I whispered in her ear.

She shook her head once, then whispered back, "Weddings make me sad, when they're not mine." Then she stifled a giggle. "Mine made me sad later."

As though sharing that confidence had lifted a burden, Sophia took a sip of her wine as the happy couple pecked each other like lovebirds doing a mating dance.

Then with the plates cleared for dessert and the bow-tie-bobbing waiter applying the crumb knife to sweep the tablecloth clean of bread crumbs and other gastronomical mishaps, Reg cleared his throat again. As he raised his wine glass, it didn't take an experienced bartender to see he was more than a little tipsy. "Harriet and I would like to invite all of you, our dear friends, to the ceremony in the captain's quarters—tomorrow night at seven."

Sophia winced. Chesty said, "That soon? Not a very long engagement, is it?"

"No," Reginald conceded, "when you're our age and you're sure, there's no point in dragging it out. At our age you never know how much time you have left—"

Probably a lot less than you would have, Harriet, if you didn't marry him, I thought. Of course, under the circumstances, I didn't think it would be too savvy to say so.

"So why waste precious time? We want to be together forever, and so we're going to do it."

"Well, I think that's just wonderful," Lillith squeaked, but she was the only one.

"So I hope you'll all come," Reginald said, then added, as though he had forgotten an important element, "Oh, and I'd like you, Gil," he turned his weird face to me, "to stand up for me. Be my best man, or witness or whatever you call it."

I just stared blankly. I tried to calculate my position.

On the one hand, I wanted nothing to do with him. I'd really had my fill. I didn't want to give him any more opportunities to stick a knife in my back. Maybe he was planning to poison my orange juice at the reception.

Then, on the other hand, there was my $150,000 fee. The closer I stayed to them, the better my chances were for keeping her alive—and the worse the chances were that I would stay alive to the end of the trip. I also realized I had to get to Harriet in the meantime to put a bat in her ear about the prenuptial agreement. Don't leave home without it.

"That's very flattering," I muttered.

"Good," Reginald said. "You accept, then."

"Well, I guess, sure. I mean what do I have to do?"

"Only be there tomorrow and sign the thing that says you saw us get married. Easy enough, eh, pal?" he said, and put his hand up on my shoulder again to show everyone what a perfectly harmless gesture that was. It would have been much easier for him to pat me on the arm, but he was intent on making his point.

Then I saw the most amazing spectacle I had ever seen on the ship. And I am not excepting the traditional baked-Alaska parade. This was a parade of another sort.

It was led by a head waiter in his black tuxedo, holding a cake with one candle in it. Behind him was the maître d', a jovial, moustached fellow who looked in his white uniform like Moby Dick. After him was a captain of the waiters who was the tiniest man on the ship. He wore a blue jacket and had to take giant steps to keep up. Behind him, the gorgeous, raven-haired female photographer, her camera hanging laconically at her side. She was in a disastrously low-backed black dress, and it was apparent the missionaries had failed to get a bead on her. Behind her marched an ancient Asian whose *schtick* was playing the trumpet, which he carried dangling like the camera ahead of him. Behind him, and bringing up the rear of this delightful parade, a young bespectacled trombonist, carrying his instrument in the cross-chest fashion as seen in lifesaving classes and the better marching bands.

The troop started at one end of the ship and came rolling down the aisle with firm and sure steps, to keep from toppling over to the roll of the ship: first the cake, then Moby Dick swinging his arms like an Italian corporal, then the Lilliputian behind him. Then the photographer leading the band, all marching in heart-stopping precision with a pomp and majesty which could never be duplicated.

They halted at our table, encircled us, and the maître d' presented the cake to Harriet. The candle had miraculously been lit somehow and now glowed on her face, turning her considerable makeup an eerie shade of amber.

Jaundice! I thought, but as usual, I kept my thoughts to myself.

Everyone took his place as though the scene were painstakingly choreographed. The dazzling photographer was in place askew from me but not so askew that I couldn't enjoy the missionaries' failure. The instrumentalists and vocalists were in a semicircle behind the celebrants so they too could be included in this memorable photo.

Then the two-piece band struck up, and our Italian chorus sang *Let Me Call You Sweetheart* in very nice English. The flash bulbs popped. Another shot was taken of the whole table with Chesty and Sophia standing behind in between the chorus and orchestra.

Their task completed, the ensemble beat a hasty and unorganized retreat.

Sophia invited me to the evening's show. I demurred. I would have my hands full trying to dope out my strategy to avoid the impending disaster. She seemed to pout, and I hastened to explain I was still recuperating from the shock of the rock.

I knew I had to finagle some way to get Harriet alone somewhere *before* the nuptials. Preferably when she was sober—which would rule out tonight. There were still ten days left on the cruise, but that could be an eternity.

15

In the morning, the engaged couple had breakfast in their room, so I did too. There was a lot of buzz about the wedding that night, as well as the little pre-dinner reception they had planned for the captain (who must have been thrilled to attend another reception) and their table mates.

I was afraid from the sound of things Reginald was planning to stick pretty close to Harriet for the balance of the day. If either had brought up the will or prenuptial agreement again, I hadn't heard it.

Then a little sunshine broke through the clouds. Harriet announced she had made an appointment to "do my hair" at two o'clock. I doubted Reginald would accompany her on that venture.

It turned out the men's sauna was adjacent to the beauty shop, so when I heard Harriet leave the room, I gave it a minute, then made my own way—in my robe and sandals (no religious cracks, please) to the men's sauna at the rear of the ship on deck nine. I peeked into the beauty salon and saw a girl in white polyester taking Harriet in tow, seating her and beginning the fuss. I went to the sauna and discovered it was at a temperature where blood would boil. Someone must have diddled with the controls, I thought. The red column in the glass was tickling 210 on the Fahrenheit scale. I was in luck.

I beat a retreat to the beauty shop to lodge my complaint. There, you'll never guess who I saw. "Harriet," I exclaimed. "How *are* you?"

"I'm fine," she said.

"Getting ready for the big night?"

"Yes, I am," she beamed. "What are you doing in this women's lair?" she asked with one of her British inflections.

"Just came to use the sauna next door. It's too hot for me. Think I'll just go in the pool instead." I was tempted to blurt it all out. I mean *everything*, about Harvey and my assignment. The only thing that held me back was my fee. I wanted it.

One of the polyester-white attendants began fussing with Harriet's head and I bade Harriet adieu, went to the front desk and asked them to please charge her treatment to my room without telling her which room I was in.

"She's getting married tonight," I explained, "I want to do it as a wedding gift."

"Very good, sir," she said, raising a highlighted eyebrow in appreciation, I suppose, of a simple looking guy like me living so high on the pig.

She showed me the bill. $120. I tried not to gulp. I signed it. I think Harvey would agree it was money well spent, though I doubted if he would reimburse me.

"So how long will she be in here?" I asked.

"Almost two hours. She's having a rinse and set, coloring, a manicure, pedicure and facial."

"When will she be sitting there waiting for the next step? I'd like to keep her company."

She looked over at Harriet and estimated, "I think about twenty minutes will be the first break. She'll have to let the color set for another twenty or so—if you want to come back then."

I went back to the sauna room and found two naked men there. That never did make me comfortable. Naked women appeal to me much more. I walked around the deck once, checked back—the white dress was still hovering, and went out to the pool area adjacent to the beauty shop. Then I walked through the "Health Spa," a room lined with machinery to give you exercise without you having to ever go anywhere. Treadmills, stationary bicycles, weights. You could walk or peddle for miles without ever having to be corrupted by the fresh ocean air.

An aerobic class was in session, loud, rocky music emanated from corner speakers. There were lots of mirrors for self-admiration, and the troops—ninety percent women—were flailing away their arms and legs. They looked like a lot of people trying to hold onto their bodies beyond the holding point.

On my next check Harriet was alone with her back to the wall, her hair slicked back and glowing with a reddish hue. I slipped into the chair next to her.

"How's it going?" I asked, without much originality.

"Necessary evil," she said. "I shouldn't be letting you watch this construction project. Men are just supposed to see the finished results of these beauty treatments. There has to be some mystery left, don't you see?"

"I promise not to look," I said.

"All right," she said as though she had won a big concession, "then you may keep me company. But if you are here to talk about what happened with Reginald the other day, I don't want to talk about it."

"I understand," I said. It was one of my favorite cop-outs. "I understand" is just about as meaningless as discourse gets. Understand what? My understanding may not be hers. I might further understand darker motives that she doesn't want understood. Then again, just because I say I understand, doesn't mean I do. "I understand," I repeated, to make it doubly bogus. "I really just want to know if there is anything I can help you with for the ceremony or anything?"

"No, thank you," she said. "That's kind of you, but it's going to be very simple, and the ship's staff has been so helpful."

"I'm glad," I said. Gladness, too, takes many forms. "How about any other details—like the agreement or something?"

"What agreement?" she asked.

"The prenuptial agreement."

"Oh," she waved me off, "I can't be bothered with those bookkeeping details right now."

"That's why I offered to help. We did talk about it, didn't we?" I was careful to keep my back to the wall and my eye on the door. I didn't want to get Reginald's hackles up again.

"Well, what if we did?" she said, "I can change my mind, can't I? It's a woman's prerogative, don't you see?"

I had promised not to look, but I snuck a glance at the red cap atop her timeworn face, and tried to *understand* her feelings. I expect she had a bit of an inferiority complex or she wouldn't pull that temperamental stuff. How many women, after all, had the strength of character to shun the beauty shop and the cosmetics industry altogether? "We are what we are," is not an adage adhered to by many women. I always thought the result of all this beauty binging made the women look silly. Oh, I could see combing your hair, but beyond that, what was the point? But I was overlooking the economics of the beauty industry. As Menken said, "No one ever went broke catering to the vanity of women."

"Harriet, I don't want to be a nag about this—but you are getting married rather suddenly, to a great guy I admit, but a guy who has had nine wives—acknowledged. Let's just say for the sake of debate that the guy decides to move on. Maybe in ten years, say when he is seventy-two and you are eighty-six. Do you want him to have a claim on your wealth?"

She pursed her shiny red lips. Lipstick did terrible things to her face. The luminous red juices worked their way into the wrinkles around her mouth so it looked like thousands of capillaries had burst, thrusting little trickles of blood away from her lips in every direction. It wasn't hard to read on those little red estuaries, the contempt Harriet had for my thoughts.

"I'm not thinking of money on my wedding day," she said. "that would be gauche, don't you see?"

"I understand," I said. "I'll take care of it for you."

"But I don't know what I want to do."

"That's okay. You don't have to. Let's just get a little insurance policy while you still have some leverage."

"Insurance policy? What in the world are you talking about? Harvey says I have enough money, I don't need insurance."

"I understand. This is a *different* kind of insurance."

"What kind?"

"Life insurance on you. Or marriage insurance, you could call it."

"How does it work?" She was trying to appear nonchalant—making small talk rather than expressing interest.

"You make an agreement with your husband-to-be that he understands that he has no claim on your trust, since it existed before you met him—"

"But I can will it to him if I want."

"Yes, and maybe in ten or fifteen years that's what you'll want to do. And if you want to be married to him that long, give him an incentive."

"What kind of incentive?" There was a touch of annoyance in her question.

"Make a prenuptial agreement that says he agrees to forgo any claims on you or your estate if he is married to you for less than ten years, or whatever you choose. You could even give him a sliding scale incentive—I wouldn't kick it in for at least five years, but that's up to you. Say after five years he'd get five percent. And each year thereafter his share would go up by another percent or two so that the longer he stays married to you, the longer you live, the more money he will get!"

"You're insulting me," she snapped.

"Why?"

"Reginald isn't marrying me for my money."

"I understand," I said. "The prenuptial agreement will prove it."

"I don't need legal documents to document our love," she said, in what I thought was a rather nice turn of phrase.

102

"I'm not trying to insult you, Harriet, but you've had a number of marriages yourself. They all began with hope and love, I'm sure. But sometimes things just change. Would you be willing to part with a lot of your money if the marriage only lasted a year?"

"You certainly are a pessimist," she said with a frown.

"Let's just look at the record. He admits to nine marriages. Do you know what the longest one was?"

"I don't care," she said.

"Two and a half years," I said. "And seven of them were less than a year."

"Why are you doing this to me? This is my wedding day. It's supposed to be a happy time for me, not a time of, of suspicion and of, of...distrust!"

"I agree," I said, "and this small document will clear it all up so there won't be suspicion or distrust or—misunderstanding."

"You are a party pooper. I don't have a lawyer, do you? Does the ship furnish lawyers?"

I shook my head. "Not necessary. A simple statement is enough—signed by both of you."

"Oh, that's so much bother, and it's out of keeping with this happy occasion."

"You have to sign the marriage license. This can't be much harder."

"But it *is*. I have to draw it up—I have to explain to Reginald that I'm more interested at this moment in protecting my money than I am in marrying him and I just won't do it."

"All right," I said, "I understand. Let me just ask you. If you did have time to think about it, how much, say, would you want Reginald to have if the unthinkable were to happen?"

"I can't think of that now. Reginald said he'd be perfectly willing to sign anything I wanted and that's good enough for me—why would he say *that* if he were after my money?"

"I'm not saying he's after your money. I'm saying if

you don't have an agreement he could get *all* your money. If that's what you want—if you want to cut out your kids, it's okay with me."

She frowned. "I just can't worry about it now," she said. "But thanks for your concern—I'll see you at the altar, six o'clock sharp—don't make us wait."

"I understand," I said.

16

"Persistence pays," Calvin Coolidge said. Napoleon said, "Victory goes to those who persevere." That was good enough for me. I went right back to my cabin to draft an agreement that they both could sign. There was a typewriter on the Norway deck. I could bang the thing out and take it to Harriet before she was finished being beautified. All I had to do was decide what it was going to say. Then it hit me that I could give them two or three options and they could choose the one most to their liking. It would give them both less excuse for welshing.

I didn't have the luxury of a lot of time to think, so I did the extremes: one where Reginald would relinquish *all* claims. I thought it astute to have that among the options because the others would then seem so much more palatable to him.

Since two and a half years was his record, I decided on three years as a minimum before he got a sou. That would keep Harriet alive well past my fee, but keeping her alive was more important to me than my fee. You understand.

While I was on the Norway deck—the one with all the public stuff—at the typewriter, I got the inspiration to make the five year minimum more attractive than the three. Kicking in at three years would be one percent the first year and a percent more for each subsequent year they held out. Going to five years I started with five percent. I suddenly realized he would have reservations about her longevity. What if he selected five years and she died in four? The risks to Harriet were obvious if these provisions were sloppy. I thought of putting in that any accidental death would preclude Reginald from ever seeing a farthing of the spoils, but I realized how touchy that might be. I think there is a law against profiting from a death that you caused—if there isn't, there should be. The problem with Bluebeard was they never found enough evidence to hang on him. My drafts would just get us to the lawyers who could put the good stuff in. My goal was to chronicle the intent of the couple in the (unlikely?) event that some tragedy occurred before they could reach a lawyer on shore.

On my way back to the beauty shop with the fruits of my laboring, I passed the usual melange of passengers in wheelchairs, on walkers, limping with canes and the occasional man or woman locomoting on his or her own steam. I passed a member of the cruise staff huddled over a table of bridge players exuding juvenile enthusiasm from every pore. It was as though these adult staff women had made a solemn pact to be as young and girly as was humanly possible; reasoning, no doubt, that the oldsters loved it.

Harriet was no longer alone when I got back to the beauty salon. That deathly smell that was part and package of the beauty shop stung my nostrils. Harriet had moved to the table at the outside wall of the ship. She could look out the window if she wanted to, but she didn't seem to want to. A white polyester was working on her. The young women in the beauty shop did not seem as girly as the cruise staff. It was more grim business here.

I hesitated only a moment before approaching Harriet at the manicure table where another white dress was caressing her fingernails. I thought at this juncture, it wouldn't hurt to have a witness.

"I took the liberty to make up three sample agreements," I said, "The ones we spoke of. You may change them anyway you like—but for everybody's sake you should both sign one of them before the wedding."

I could tell from her face that Harriet was seething inside. She looked at the manicurist as if to see if her stock had been watered in the servant's eyes. The round, dark-haired woman worked away on the mistress's nails as though she were deaf.

"Why do you persist at this?" Harriet asked, her zigzag red lips tightening.

I thought of telling her what Cal Coolidge said, but decided against it.

"It's none of your business, really," she said.

"Yes," I said. "I understand. But Reginald did ask me to take a major part in your ceremony so I take my responsibilities seriously. That is plugging up these loose ends that neither of you have time for—but are vital to *your* well-being. I'll just put them in your purse and you can look at them when you get back to your cabin."

"Oh all right," she said. "If I must."

I thanked her out of proportion to my debt, and as I moseyed in a daze back to my cabin, I realized she would probably not even mention the documents to Reginald.

In my cabin, I played the tape on the chance that I missed some conversation. I had not. I lay down on the bed listening for the ping of the door next door. I must have drifted off to sleep because when I next thought of my neighbors, they were conversing next door. I picked their discussion up in progress.

"He what?"

"Says we should have an agreement before we marry."

"What does he have to do with it?"

"I don't know. I wondered too."

"I told you I'd do whatever you want." There was a pause. "I don't know about what *Gil* wants. I really don't care about pleasing him, but I do care about you. I want to make you happy. Just tell me what it takes."

There was another silence during which I had top hopes Harriet was giving serious consideration to the agreement. It was only broken by the clinking of ice cubes from the ice bucket the butler replenished three times a day, followed by the blub, blub, blub of pouring liquid.

"Here you go, Honeycakes, a pick-me-up."

"Thank you, dear."

"Here's to you," he said; "here's to us. May we have a long and happy life together."

"A-men." she said.

"God, your hair looks smashing," he oozed. "You look like a teenager, you know it?"

"Oh, Reginald, don't you say the nicest things—"

"Well I mean them."

There was another silence. Then, "Where did I put them...?"

"What?"

"Those agreements Gil drew up," she said.

"I'll sign anything, doll. If you want me to jump overboard, just put it in writing. The way I feel about you, I'd sign anything."

"Well, that might be a little drastic, don't you think?"

"Nothing's too drastic for you, babe."

"Here they are," she said. "Why don't you just look at them and see what you think."

"Sure, doll."

There was a prolonged silence during which even *I* was uncomfortable. I heard more ice cubes clink. More blub, blub, blub. Then another silence.

"Geez, babe," he said finally, "I am frank to admit this high finance is way beyond me. I was a two-bit con, this is professional caliber."

"You mean these agreements are a con?"

"Well, I don't know. What would you call them? Hey, I told you, I'll sign anything. Why don't I just put my John Hancock on the one that says I'll get zilch? But that wouldn't be strictly accurate because I'm getting you, and I only wish I had a hundred billion dollars to give to you for marrying me because I'd gladly give you all I have. But I'm unfortunately not in that position, so I come to you more or less as a pauper and a beggar. But I'm only begging for your most fantastic love, not for your money. Shakespeare said 'Who steals my purse steals trash,' and that's just how I feel about it now—I'm sixty-two—I've conned for pennies all my life. I made good money, I didn't need it, but it was this stupid challenge. I've finally outgrown it, and my only regret is I have to live on your money, and if, God forbid, anything should happen to you, why I'll just go get a job. I don't know what that would be offhand, because if I should outlive you, I'll be a very old man when you go, and I wasn't in a line of work that pays social security, but that's no reason to even think about me. I'll manage. Here, let me freshen your drink."

"Thank you, Reginald."

There was another silence during which I thought I heard some more ice cubes clinking.

"Is Gil a lawyer, babe?"

"I told you he wasn't."

"Then how does he know these things are legal?"

"They are just agreements. When we get back home we can have my lawyer draw up something more."

"Yeah, that's a good idea. I'd feel a lot better about that." He spoke as though that ended it. My heart sank.

"But he thinks, Gil, that is, thinks my children would get nothing if something happened to me before we got home."

"Happen?" he said with an angry astonishment. "What could happen to you in two weeks? I'm right with you, I don't intend to leave your side. I'd die before I let anything happen to you."

"That's sweet of you," she said. "But we never know, do we? I'm not a spring chicken you know, and I have been a terrible procrastinator about doing a will. You are such a wonderful, vigorous lover, who knows? I could have a heart attack in bed."

"Nonsense. That happens to men, not women."

"But doesn't it seem easy to make us all feel better?"

"Easy? You mean signing? Sure, nothing easier. Just

tell me which one to sign."

"I don't care, really. Just so my children don't lose everything."

"Good idea. They certainly deserve something."

"They *are* my children after all, don't you see?"

"Sure I do. Do you have a pen? I think it will be good for little Harvey to get a lot of money. He's never really been able to earn any on his own. This should finally make a man out of him."

"I'm not sure about that, Reginald dear. I'm going to give all that more thought when we get home. This is only a temporary measure…"

"In case you pop off in the next two weeks."

"Yes."

"You don't think I'd try to hurt you?"

"Of course not."

"Then what are you worried about?"

"Oh, Reginald, I'm not worried. Let's not argue on our wedding day. If you don't want to sign it, don't."

"Well, I'd feel better if a lawyer did it right from the beginning. But, hey, I'll sign if you want."

There was a silence during which I died 1,119 deaths. I thought the great retired, ex-con had made his greatest con.

"I would be grateful," she said in a small voice so quiet that I almost didn't hear it.

"Sure. No problem," he said with a lot of forced bravado. Even that came over on the tape. "No problem at all. Do you have a pen, doll?"

"No, I…"

"There must be one around here someplace."

The sounds of rummaging about the cabin permeated my earphones. Strange, I thought, there were pens all over the place, courtesy of the cruise line. Finally—

"Here, I got one," he said. "Now what did I do with those papers?"

"There on coffee table, dear. There, in front of you."

"Oh yeah. Good. Great! So which one will it be?"

"Why don't you decide," she said.

"No, I want you to. I'm the beggar here," he said in what I detected to be a petulant tone. "You call the tune."

"Reginald, I *don't* think of you as a beggar. This is just really a precaution to protect my children since I've been a bad mother about this."

"Sure, well, yeah. Good all. Which one? I insist you pick. You don't pick, I don't sign."

"Well, I don't know very much about these things—"

"Amen," he interrupted her, "I don't either. Maybe a lawyer—"

"But since you mentioned that about maybe having a hard time finding work when you are older, why doesn't it seem like it would be good to sign one of these where you *do* get money. One is after three years, the other after five gives more of course, but we'd have to be married longer."

"No problem, doll, we're going to be married forever."

"I hope so," she said. "What I was saying was you won't have to worry if we last three years. If we don't, you'll still be young enough to work."

"So it's the three year one you want."

"Or the five. You'd get more in five—"

"Oh, I can't think of these things now. I'm too caught up in my love for you—"

"Please, let's just do it and not talk anymore about it."

"Which one."

"Here, take these two and shuffle them behind your back then bring one front and sign it. if you really have no preference."

"Okay," he said. I heard the shuffle. Then he brought one forward. "Three years," he said. "Fair enough."

I was sure he had faked the shuffle. He knew which one he was signing.

17

Captain Sunderstrom and the Regal Cruise Lines put on a gala wedding for Harriet and Reginald. Gala was the big operative word on the ship denoting any event as the cat's nightgown.

The captain's living room, or captain's quarters, were so named because they took up a quarter of the ship. Well, not really, but his living room, which he graciously offered for the wedding, was the size of two penthouses. On the front wall (bow wall, I guess) were glass cabinets with tasteful tourist souvenirs from various ports of call: a carved and polished pygmy, a glass Eskimo in a kayak and other stuff, which if they paid less for, we would call junk. But these nicknacks they would say were museum quality.

They also gave the captain nice, dark mahogany wood for his walls to get the place to look as much like a swank men's club as possible.

Pandering to protocol, I got there first. Then Beefy came in with his bride and made a B-line for the leather couch against the wall. Chester Brown was a man who had perfected the art of sitting, a man who took to heart the sage advice: Never stand when you can sit. Sitting down, he looked like the folds on an intestine slumped in a jar of formaldehyde. His wife was prim and upright next to him, sitting with her feet flat on the floor, her knees together and her hands flat on top of those knees. Looking at this unlikely couple, you couldn't help get the feeling they were saying

"All right, go ahead, amuse us." And from the look of them, the rest of us seldom succeeded at that.

Beefy wore his medium-blue suit which he wore on formal nights such as this one, and Lillith was in her favorite peach-colored, full-length, simple-but-feminine poly-blend. Sophia came in next, moving as though she were on roller skates with a flowing, flouncing skirt and wildly contrasting fitted top, which was fitted of course on that part of her body that was the real McCarthy.

Then the captain came in. He was a blond guy with glasses in a white uniform. I told him it was awfully good of him to do this for the couple, and he said, "I enjoy it, I wouldn't have this job if I didn't enjoy it." His English was accomplished, though they had not taken the Norwegian country accent out of the boy.

As though on key, Reginald and Harriet came through the wide door leading to the captain's lair. Reginald looked thinner in his tux, his forehead glistening from the captain's overhead lights. Harriet seemed more frail and unsteady, and I knew from my auditing that it had taken a lot of ice clinking and blub, blub, blubbing to bring her here tonight.

She was wearing a silk thing, pale blue in hue, which revealed shoulders which might have been better covered up. Perhaps I was reading my own emotions into her, but I thought she looked more frightened than happy, more anxious than serene.

Reg came right for me, took my insubstantial bicep in his Hell's Angel hand and squeezed the sunlights out of it. "Thanks for your great help with the prenuptial agreement," he said into my ear. "I really appreciate it." The blood stopped dead in my arm, and I had nothing to do but wait for my hand and forearm to drop to the floor.

I nodded. What else could I do? I couldn't speak.

When he finally released me, I noted through half-closed eyes that Reginald was smiling from ear to Texas, and I fought valiantly the impulse to faint.

The captain filled us in on the flitty gritty of the ceremony—who stood where and who did what. He assured us that with the customary ship's precision the reception goodies would magically appear at the appointed moment, putting a somewhat nervous Harriet somewhat at ease.

The mumbo jumbo began. The celebrated couple stood facing the captain (who was not married himself. What was that about not making the rules if you don't play the game?) I was next to Reginald where he could again cut off my blood circulation should the fancy strike him.

The other three were seated on the couch facing the goings-on.

The captain read from a booklet with his charming Norwegian inflection, with appropriate, tight smiles at regular intervals, whether the text called for them or not. It was as though along with the words there were stage directions for grim smiles. Then, too, perhaps the captain had a sense of the sense or nonsense of this marriage.

He was thoughtful enough to ask the assembled strangers if any of us had reservations about joining these two anonymous figures together in holy matrimony, and it does us no credit that each and every one of us kept our mouths shut.

As the captain rang down the curtain on the nuptial procedures the bride and groom engaged in an embarrassing smooch, and the formalities were over. The captain then produced the coveted marriage certificate for both parties to sign. Reginald signed first, then while his new bride was signing, he asked the captain, "Is this all we get—one copy?"

"That's the standard," he said. "We will send the original to the states, to California, where they will keep it on record."

"Could I get some extra copies?"

"You could photocopy all you want."

"No, I mean extra originals."

"They would have to be marked 'copy'," the captain said. "There can only be one 'original'."

"Okay—do that. Mark them copy."

The captain had now been put into the position of Reginald's errand boy and I thought I saw him bridle a bit. "How many would you like, one more?"

"Make it five, captain," he said, as though he were talking, none too tactfully, to a waiter.

"I'll see to it," the captain said. "They will be delivered to your cabin."

"I'll look for them—" Reginald said. "Oh, and captain?"

"Yes?"

"Thanks." Reginald was already acting nouveau riche.

"My pleasure."

All life is deception.

On cue, the troops rolled in with the canapés and champagne and we all got festive.

The bride, feeling no pain when she came in, got positively swacked at the reception, and I observed how Reginald Windsor, the lucky bridegroom, drank much less and was able to keep his head about him. Of course that was not good news to yours sincerely who was charged with keeping this woman alive.

One would not think that the bride would be in danger on her wedding night, but I realized I could not draw another comfortable breath until she was safe at home. I assumed that when she boarded the plane, she would be safe. But Old Beefy told me never to assume.

The captain wished the happy couple all his best and made some excuses about duty calling and disappeared, leaving us guests in his home without a host. It made for a slightly uncomfortable feeling, but we persevered.

"Gil, how about giving us a toast?" Reginald said, catching me off guard. Since I didn't drink, I was not up on toasts. I wanted to give him that excuse but realized it was a command performance and was also probably part of the expected duties of the best man. May the best man win, I thought. I'd better say something nice and something soon. With no preparation, I stumbled.

I hoisted my glass of ginger ale. The others followed with whatever was in their glasses. "Here is to the lucky couple. I don't know much about them, but I think they each know what they want. May that always coincide with what the other wants. Here's to their long and happy life together."

"Hear, hear!" Reginald chimed in and took a very small swallow though he seemed to take more. Harriet took a big, undisguised swallow of her drink. She was almost mannish with her drinking gesture. Ordinarily she was very dainty. But the tying of this proverbial bow seemed to have emboldened her. I only hoped it wouldn't make her careless.

"I have a toast, too," she said, in a peculiar Scottish accent. She lifted her cut-crystal glass, then noticed it was almost empty.

"Waiter," she called out imperiously, "I need more champagne!" and it was promptly provided. Blub, blub, blub.

The glass went back up.

> "Hare's to us.
> Whare's lak us?
> Oooll dead.
> Mare's the pity!"

A generous round of appreciative applause followed, and Harriet beamed. "Your turn, Reg," she said. "Come on."

"Gosh," he said. "I'm too shy in front of all these people."

"Dear friends all," she said.

"Yes," he said, "a good starting point." He lifted his glass which was virtually full, in spite of several passes at taking big gulps, and said, "Dear friends all. What Gil said was true, we don't know much about each other—but," he said as though it were an afterthought, "maybe we know too much." He looked at me meaningfully and there was a titter of appreciation among the assembled guests. Reginald beamed with satisfaction. "Seriously, though, today I am a happy man. I am so grateful Harriet accepted my proposal. I have never been happier. Every day I am with her I feel like a better man. She would have been willing to wait, but I rushed her. When you get to be our age, you shouldn't be wasting time. I've wasted too much time already. I'm not that proud of my profligate past. But I am going to be proud of my productive future. I'm going to stay by Harriet's side till death do us part. And if I could have one wish, it would be that that day never come. I love ya, babe," and he threw his glass back to gulp another sip. Then he put his arm around Harriet and gave her another kiss.

Old Beefy spoke up from the couch where he had been sitting inert like a beached whale, "What's this about a profligate past?"

"Oh, I don't want to talk about it," Reginald said. "Not today. I'm turning over a new leaf. That's all behind me. I've told my sweetheart all about it and she's married me anyway, and I'll be grateful as long as I live."

Or as long as she lives, I thought.

"Think you can teach an old dog new tricks?" Beefy asked.

"I don't know about other dogs," Reginald said, "but this dog's committed." And he gave Harriet another kiss.

Someone else was committed as a result of this marriage. Me. I was almost surprised to see Reginald didn't mention the prenuptial agreement. Here was a master at his game. When the situation called for deceit, he was the master of deception. When the situation seemed to call for a clean breast of things, you couldn't find a cleaner breast. But always with qualifications—with caveats. He was writing the script. He would play on his points. He would make himself seem the super-devoted husband interested in long-term marriage, long life for both. He wouldn't mention the agreement because that was to appear as utterly unimportant to him. Not even worth the mention. And if he didn't mention it, that many fewer people would know about it when it came time to refer to it—when, shucks, he forgot where he put it—but he remembered what it said. Then it would be anybody's guess what he'd say. If he were smart he would satisfy Harvey with a generous cut, assuming Harvey could be satisfied with anything less than the whole tamale. And you know what Chester 'Old Beefy' Brown had to say about assuming. Because if he did manage to 'lose' the agreement and she died intestate without anyone being able to pin anything on him, Mr. Reginald Windsor a.k.a. Fred Kantor would be a very rich man. And I would have flunked my fee.

I had to get my hands on a copy of the agreement.

We trickled down to dinner a half-hour late. I made excuses to Gorge, our waiter, and told him we had a wedding ceremony. He bobbed his bow tie.

When we were all seated—Reginald had insisted I stay by his side the entire evening, then made some joke about "well, not the entire evening, pal."—Reginald ordered us some more heavy duty hooch. One or two more drinks later poor Harriet was so tipsy I thought she would collapse into her soup. But she managed to keep her chin up, albeit barely, for the rest of the celebration. But it must have been obvious to everyone she was getting the lioness' share of the vino.

Before the dessert was served, the waiter produced a package as apparently prearranged—and set it on the table in front of Reginald. He in turn presented it to his bride. "I bought you a wedding present."

"Oooo, you shouldn't have," she said. "Did you charge it to the room?"

"Well, ah, yes…but—"

"Then I bought me a wedding present," she tittered in her cup.

"But I'll pay it back."

"How will you do that? Are you planning to inherit some money?"

Holy smokes, I thought. She said just what I was thinking and the natural result was for all the table to steam up some sympathy for poor Reginald. He meant so well, and he tried so hard, but she just had a penchant for cutting him off at the knees.

He blushed. "You know I'll get a job if you want me to. I've always been able to work."

"We'll see," she said, and tore into the package. It was a camera. She stared at it as though it were an invention unknown to her.

"It's a camera," he helped her out. "We can record the trip, our honeymoon."

"But I don't know how to work these things," Harriet said.

"It's easy," Reginald said, "I'll help you."

"Too bad we didn't have it sooner," she said.

"I took some pictures," Sophia said. "I'll have them developed and give them to you—my wedding present."

"How nice," Reginald said. "Thank you very much."

"I didn't see you taking any pictures," Harriet said.

"Good. I wanted to be inconspicuous. If there's anything I hate it's one of those weddings where the photographer is always in your face."

"I hope you didn't take any of me in profile."

"I don't think I took anything that looked bad," Sophia hedged, "but if I did you can just throw them away."

That got Harriet's back up. A lot of things did. "Don't worry, I will," she said.

That camera, I thought, would bode no good.

For dessert we got another cakewalk parade with the maître d', the captain, headwaiter, the gorgeous photographer with a green velveteen that clung intimately to her perfect body as it turned hither and thither. The tired trumpeter and the young trombonist brought up the rear.

They formed the duty bound semicircle and sang again:

> "Let me call you sweetheart,
> I'm in love with you.
> Let me hear you whisper

that you love me too.
Keep the love light glowing
In your eyes so blue.
Let me call you sweetheart,
I'm in love with you."

This time it sounded like a dirge.
I was not in a very festive frame of mind.

18

There was, as you might imagine, a hot time in the old cabin tonight. Bluebeard was no piker, I had to give him that. He not only flattered the pants off Harriet, but once they were off he knew what to do. I don't care how many times I heard the goings on next door, I never got used to it. I tried to understand how it could be done with the principals involved (not to say principles), and the state of their consciousness, but I never conquered it. And it *always* embarrassed me.

After that, we all had a good night's sleep.

In the morning, they had breakfast in their room, so I did the same. And why not? It was the nicest room on the ship—excepting maybe the captain's quarters which served as the wedding chapel. But that was a little too large for my taste. I have decided it is better to keep your tastes more modest. Like the guy who said he didn't like those fancy, expensive cars, and the other guy said, "I can't afford one either."

Through the earphones I heard Reginald was able to prolong the cootchie-coo talk through to the morning after the wedding night. The ship was floating on calmer waters again, and I hoped that was an omen for the marital union.

Having realized the flaw in my otherwise successful prenuptial agreement ploy, I concentrated on a plan to rectify it. How was I going to get a copy? Failing that, a copy sent to Harvey or given to the captain or even Old Beefy would serve the purpose. As it was, that agreement in Reginald's possession was pretty worthless. How difficult would it be for a guy who killed his wife to destroy a piece of paper? In the meantime, he would be in possession of five copies of the marriage license, probably in safe-deposit boxes and various other safe repositories throughout the free world.

"Dear," Reginald was saying through my earphones that were picking up the conversations from their penthouse next to mine, "I meant what I said last night about staying with you. I feel so bound up to you I don't *ever* want to be away from you."

"Let's not get carried away," she said. "We're both going to need our time alone."

"Not on the honeymoon," he said. "People aren't alone on their honeymoons."

"Oh, Reginald, you're such a hopeless romantic."

"Yeah, I confess," he said, "I am. Want to take some pictures? I'm excited about the camera. I want to take a thousand pictures of you."

"Well, I guess if it's only of me. I never did learn how to work a camera so I won't be able to take you."

"Who'd want to see me anyway? *You're* the beautiful one."

"Oh, Reginald, you say the sweetest, silliest things. You'd think I was a twenty-year old."

"To me you *are*," Reginald said, "and always will be."

"You're sweet."

A silence. Then, he said, "So what shall we do today? Movies, Trivial Pursuit, bingo?"

"Ugh..."

"Look, here's something new."

"What?"

"Skeet shooting."

My heart sank.

"Skeet shooting?"

"Yeah, you ever done it?"

122

"No!"

"I haven't either. Might be fun. Wanna try it?"

"Not particularly. I wouldn't even know how to hold a gun."

"Well, they'll show you."

"No, thanks."

"Would you go with me while I do it?"

"Oh, Reginald, why?"

"So we can be together on our honeymoon."

"How long does it take?"

"I don't know. Not much more than a half-hour, I guess."

"You can be alone for a half-hour," she said. "What would I do while you are shooting anyway?"

"You could watch me. Give me pointers—moral support," he said. "You'd give me inspiration."

"But you're an athlete," she said. "I'm not. And I don't have the slightest interest in guns."

"Okay babe, then I won't go," he said. "Just an idea."

"Isn't that silly? You want to do it, do it. Just because I don't wan—"

"No, no. I don't have to. I just thought it might be fun. If you don't want to do it, *I* don't want to either. I want to be with you."

"Now, isn't that silly?"

"Not to me."

"All right," she said. "if you are going to be a child about it, I'll go with you."

My old heart sank again, but what did I expect? She was in the hands of a master.

"You sure?"

"I'm sure."

"Okay, doll, you make me so happy. I can use the new camera."

"What for?"

"To take some pictures of you with the gun."

"But I'm not going to shoot."

"You don't have to. I'll do the shooting. You can take a picture of me."

"But I don't know *how* to take pictures."

"I'll set it up. All you have to do is push a button."

That ended the discussion, and my hopes for a peaceful, unthreatening first day of the marriage. Of course, I could focus on the skeet shoot, there probably wouldn't be any funny business until that. Just in case, I would stay with them—as out of sight as possible—in the hope I could get Harriet alone to press my case for the copies of the prenuptial agreement.

"Let's walk the deck, Mrs. Windsor," Reginald said. "I just love calling you Mrs. Windsor. I'm so glad I could give you a royal name befitting your aristocratic person. It's a name befitting someone whose ancestors came over on the Mayflower."

"Yes, isn't that lucky," she said.

"Ready?"

"Oh, I don't know. I'm a little tired," she said. "I should have known marrying such a younger man would take its toll."

"Come on, doll. Keeping up will keep you young."

"Oh, all right. You are a hard man to say no to, you know?"

In a few minutes they were out and about and so was I. They went to the shops in the center of the Norway deck and from my discreet, hidden distance, I got the sense that he wanted to buy her something and she didn't want him to. Already he seemed to take a proprietary interest in her checkbook.

From there they headed for the area that was flooded with bridge players, then into the Midnight Sun Lounge, where some women were doing needlepoint under the watchful, and oh-so-appreciative, eye of the pretty social director. Then they made their way to the other end of the ship where a tall, thin professor was professing about the sociological makeup of the South Sea islands. That engaged their interest until it was almost lunch time. The balance of their leisure was killed sitting in the Oak Room—the same place he tried to strangle me—having a drink.

I didn't want a repeat of that scene so I went to lunch ahead of Reginald and Harriet in the hope of seeing Sophia Romanoff before the others. Luckily, as soon as I sat down, Sophia magically appeared. I needed an accomplice, and due to my circumscribed life aboard this ship, I didn't know anyone except the folks at our table. Somehow I couldn't see gruff-and-ready Chesty Brown doing me much good. Subtlety was not a bullet in his quiver. His wife seemed nice enough, but sometimes talked like she didn't have both oars in the water.

When I presented my plan to Sophia, she said, "Sure, I'll help you out. He reminds me of my ex—I got nothing but sympathy for Harriet."

"Would you tell her I'd like to see her alone for five minutes? Today. Very important, *today!*" I said.

"Yeah, well sure. Can I tell her what for?"

"It's about Harvey, her son. And her daughter."

"Why do you need her alone?"

"Sensitive subject with the bridegroom. I don't want to risk another choking."

"I'll see what I can do," Sophia said. "When she goes to the bathroom, I'll try to distract Reginald. You can grab her then. But don't take too long, I always get nervous with this clandestine stuff."

She always went to the bathroom when she drank, so I offered to buy them a bottle of wine at lunch, an offer that was not refused. Just before dessert, she excused herself and Sophia, who had sat next to Reginald, started bending his ear.

I slipped quietly away from the table, looking up at the ceiling as if I had not a care in the world. I waited in the elevator corridor between dining rooms for Harriet to emerge from the door with the little gold plaque that said:

LADIES

I hadn't waited long when she appeared in a flattering (believe it or not) rose pink shirt dress, that I noticed for the first time. "Oh ho, Harriet," I hailed her. "How does it feel to be a married woman?"

"Oh, I don't know," she said. "It is not exactly a new feeling for me, don't you know?"

"How did you make out with the prenuptial agreement?" I asked outright. She could make it back to the table in seconds, and if I didn't get right to the point I would miss my opportunity. But her back seemed to go rigid as she said through suspicious eyes, "All right."

"He signed one of them?"

"Yes he did," she said with her back up to Napoleon proportions.

"What have you done with it?"

"We have them."

"Would it be better to give one to me—or to mail it to Harvey?"

"Maybe I'll do that when we get to port."

"You can give it to the desk now and they'll mail it when we get in."

She looked at me like I'd rather not be looked at. "Why do *you* care so much about this?"

"I feel I should protect you. I can afford to be paranoid where perhaps you can't. It's just an insurance. A lot of Reginald's wives died accidentally. You could too, I suppose. Suddenly. This will just prove he didn't do it—*If* someone besides him has a copy."

"Well I really don't think it is any more business of yours, thank you."

"Please. Don't give it to me. Give it to the captain, the concierge, anyone—Don't, please, have an accident."

"So what if his wives had accidents? My husbands did too, and I certainly had nothing to do with them. Old people have accidents."

"I hope you aren't one of them."

She started back to the table. "Please Mr. Yates, I must ask you to mind your own affairs."

"All right. Just think about it, please."

"I'll talk to Reginald."

"Good. Watch his reaction."

"Mr. Yates—*please*," she said, and marched back in—Napoleon going into Russia, not coming out.

I wanted to skip dessert, but I was afraid if I weren't there to inhibit them, they would talk of the prenup without my hearing any of it.

19

It was back at the table that Harriet thanked me for picking up the beauty shop tab. "Wasn't that nice of him?" she asked Reginald. She loved rhetorical questions.

All the conversation was circumspect, and the only distraction I experienced was Princess Sophia Romanoff squeezing my hand under the table.

I high-tailed it back to the cabin when I saw the newlyweds headed that way. I put on my earphones and didn't have long to wait until my private entertainers returned and began their discourse about which one was most interested in the other.

"My God," Reginald said. "What took you so long in the bathroom? That Sophia person talked the leg off me."

"I'm sorry, dear, if I had known. She is such an unpleasant bore, isn't she?"

"She's a decent person I guess, but I don't want to spend that kind of time with her. What took you so long?"

"I met Gil Yates in the hall."

"Gil? In the ladies room?"

"In the *hall*, I said."

"So?"

"He started a conversation."

"About what?"

"The prenuptial agreement."

"He certainly has taken an unusual interest in our affairs hasn't he? What's his problem now?"

"He says he's concerned no one has a copy but us."

"Who else needs one? The waiter? The stewardess? Perhaps we should publish it in the ship's newspaper. Is he trying to announce to the world *you* have the money? Is that it?" He was building up some steam.

"I don't know. He says if something happens to me and nobody has a copy of the agreement you could destroy it."

"But why would I do that?"

"Because then I guess he thinks you would inherit all my money."

"Does he think *he* would get it otherwise?"

She laughed, a short, concise, objective laugh. The nervous laugh of one unaccustomed to any other kind.

"Because his meddling is starting to get old, if you ask me. Who the hell does he think he is? I underwent the indignity of signing the thing that makes it look like I was only marrying you to get at your money, so we needed that ridiculous paper to prove I wasn't a mercenary crook. And now that we have it, it's not enough, we have to publish it!" His voice was up there in the high dudgeon register.

"Oh, Reginald, he doesn't want to publish it. Just wants someone to have a copy. Says it is for our protection."

"*Our* protection. How does that protect me, pray tell?"

"Well, you do get a percentage. It's not like you would be cut out or anything."

"Yes and *I* had to sign it. I had to be humiliated by this meddling crybaby, and I can't for the life of me understand what *he* has to do with it."

"He just brought it up is all."

"So what did you tell him?"

"I told him it was none of his business."

"Good for you!" he shouted.

"But I guess it is *our* business."

"What? You want to give *him* a copy? I'm so damn mad at him how—this is what I get for befriending him—a sock in the jaw—a kick in the shins."

"Oh, Reg, it's not so bad."

"Bad! It's an insult. He's making it look like my motives are tarnished. I won't have anymore of it! I'm fed up with his pushy, nosy meddling in our lives! Tell him to buzz off."

"You tell him."

"By damn, I will!"

"Well, you needn't get so angry about it."

"Damn it," he swore. "I'm mad!"

"Are you so mad you won't let *any*one see a copy?"

"What's the point? I'll put them in the safe in the closet. Nobody can get to them there."

There was now a silence, during which I hoped Harriet would be thinking about the ramifications of hiding the documents in the safe. All he had to do was go to the safe and destroy them. Surely she didn't need *me* to remind her of that. Don't give up Harriet, I pleaded to myself. Don't give up!

"Will putting them in the safe solve the problem?" she asked in a small voice.

"Problem?" He was irritated. "What's the problem?"

"Oh, Reg, we've been all *over* this. You know what his fear is. Why do you keep pretending you don't?"

"I *don't* know," he said. "I guess I'm just so god-damn mad I can't see straight. It's bad enough not being able just to dump a couple million dollars on you, and if I had it, believe me, nothing would make me happier. Now since I don't have it, everyone wants to rub my nose in it. Publicize it. Well, I resent it, and I'm damn mad at that wimp. Jesus, I made him my best man for Christ's sakes! What kind of friend did he turn out to be?"

"Oh, Reg, he's only thinking of me."

"You? Why you? He doesn't even know you—or does he?"

"No, of course not. I never saw him before in my life," she said. "Reginald. Why are you looking at me that way, don't you believe me?"

"I did. I believed you always told me the truth. Now

I'm wondering."

"Why?"

"Because it doesn't make sense. Here's a stranger who knows nothing about us, all of a sudden he's in the middle of our most private things. I don't get it, frankly."

"Well, for one thing," she said, "He's not a perfect stranger to us. We both talked to him. We both told him about our pasts, so I guess he's a sensitive person who took an interest in me. Then when you asked him to be your best man, he started to take it more seriously. That may be just the sort of person he is, don't you think?"

"All I know is I don't want anything more to do with him. I'm going to talk to the maître d' about moving us to another table. I wouldn't miss any of those geeks, would you?"

"I don't know about that. I've become accustomed to them. I don't know if I want to take my chances and start all over," she said. "Look, Reg, can't we solve this? Can't we agree on one person to give a copy of the agreement to? I'm willing for it to be anybody."

"No, damn it. I want to please you, but this is just getting on my nerves. If you don't trust me, I'll get off in Aukland and you can keep your prenuptial agreement—though it will be postnuptial by then."

"Is that the way you feel?" she asked.

I don't know if he nodded or what, but there was a long excruciating silence during which I was experiencing a variety of pains.

"Well, I guess if that's the way you feel," she said at last.

"It is."

"Well, I hope you'll change your mind. I'll be sorry to lose you."

I jumped for joy and the cord on the earphones snapped me back to reality—as did the voice of Bluebeard:

"Hey, wait a minute, babe, is that all I mean to you?"

"Apparently that is all *I* mean to *you*," she said. "It was your idea, remember. In the meantime, I'll give the agreement to Gil to hold."

"Hey wait a minute!"

"Because I am just feeling a little peculiar about this, don't you see?"

"No. I—"

"Well, I just never expected this kind of incensed reaction from you. You've always been so kind and considerate of my every move. Even when I've been mean and unpleasant, you've been the soul of restraint. This is a side of you I've just never seen, and frankly my dear, it scares me."

"Oh, babe, no. No, I'm sorry. I'm being overly sensitive. Of course you have concerns and so you should. My past hasn't been that exemplary. So what will it take, Honeycakes, a full page ad in the *New York Times*? Go for it. We'll publish the whole thing."

"Oh, Reg—"

"No, really. Isn't that what you want?"

"No it is not. I just want someone not connected to us to have a copy."

"Gil is connected by now."

"All right, give it to someone else."

"Who?"

"The captain—"

"Why would he mess with something like this?"

"Mail it to Harvey."

"Take too long. We could deliver it before he'd get it in the mail from here."

"I've suggested two, now you suggest two."

"I can't think of two. I can't even think of one," he said. There was a gestation pause. Then he said, "I suppose we could give it to one of those people at the table."

"All right."

"I just...I don't know, sitting there for the rest of the cruise having them know our business and knowing they know...I just don't like it."

"Someone at another table?"

"Nah. I guess it's okay. We could seal it in an envelope and put on the outside not to be opened unless one of us dies."

She didn't argue with the "one of us," though she must have known it was only germane if *she* died.

"I suppose," he continued, "we should give it to that ridiculous woman. I can't bear the thought of Chester Brown and his wife having it. He'd tear into it the moment our backs were turned. Besides, two people would know instead of one. What do you think?"

"I think you're right. I'm not crazy about Sophia, but I'm satisfied."

"Good," he said. "Then you can give it to her so you'll be satisfied."

"Oh, Reg—"

"No, no, it's okay. I'm okay with it. I just think it shows a major distrust of me, but I'll get over it. Once she has it, I hope we can forget about it."

"I do too, dear," she said. "Is there an envelope around here somewhere?"

20

"Skeet shooting time!" Reginald announced in my earphones.

"Oh, I forgot. Did I agree to do that barbaric thing with you?"

"You sure did."

"Shall we get the envelope to Sophia first?"

"Let's give it to her at dinner. No sense making a big to-do about it. I love you, babe."

There was a great kissing sound. "I love you, too."

The skeet shooting was on the back of the promenade deck on the starboard side of the ship—I was out there minutes before they were, and I was nervous as all get out.

A Philippine sailor was bolting to the handrail the device that threw the clay circles charmingly called "clay pigeons" out over the ocean. I asked him, "Is this at all dangerous?"

"No," he said. "We shoot over the water."

"Never been an accident?"

"No."

"Are they real bullets?"

"Shotgun, yes."

"Could they hurt somebody?"

"If you shot somebody, sure. But we are shooting these clay birds."

"But suppose someone turned and fired at a person.

Would he—or she—die?"

"Well, if he got hit right, yes. But we don't do that."

"How do you control that?"

"I am here, an officer is here. But if someone wants to shoot someone, why do it here with witnesses?"

"To make it look like an accident," I said.

"Oh," he said with a frown. "We will be careful."

Then I saw Reginald and Harriet come out the door and turn toward us in the stern.

"Yates," he said scowling, "You a shooter?"

"I don't know. Never did, but I'm curious. I may watch and try it later. You?"

"Yeah, I love it."

"Any good?"

"Not bad."

"I don't even know how it works."

"Little machine there flips the pigeon in the sky after the shooter says 'pull'. Then he shoots, leading it a little. The object is to hit the clay bird and shatter it. Fun."

"I'll watch, if you don't mind."

"Suit yourself," he said. Now I was wondering if I might be a target for him myself. Then I felt that ubiquitous ham hand circle my biceps and apply the old pressure as he pulled me out of earshot of his wife.

"Listen, Yates," he said with his friendly-menacing tone, "Harriet is a bit put out at your sticking your nose in our business. I said I'd talk to you about it, so consider this it. I know you have a heart of gold and mean the best for all concerned, she just thinks it's so unseemly. So be a little seemly will you, pal? We can look out for ourselves, dig?"

I think I might have fainted for the rest of it, if there was a rest of it. I remember feeling a rebirth when the hand was suddenly released. And the remarkable thing I remember was Reggie smiling benignly the whole time, just as though we were having the most wonderful, friendly chat.

My brain needed that blood that stopped flowing when Reg squeezed my arm. I had very unpleasant visions and no idea how to cope. One thing was certain, I didn't have the requisite courage or reflexes for the Secret Service. I just couldn't imagine myself throwing my only body in front of a bullet that was intended for someone else. But if you think about it, has any secret service man ever taken a bullet meant for a president? How could you? Those bullets are fast. Faster than any human. But the idea was not something I could get my arms around. It was a whacko way to make a living. Even if I wanted to, I didn't think I had the reflexes for it.

An officer came down the deck carrying two shot-guns, single-barreled. Good Lord, I thought, the Windsors are going to have a duel. I knew I couldn't take the bullet, but what could I do? Watch closely, I guess. The prenuptial was still in Reginald's hands. It had not been given to Sophia, as far as I knew. I stood back wondering—trying to calculate what would happen. Would he really have the nerve to shoot her with all these witnesses? It didn't appear anyone else was interested in skeet shooting today, but there was still the officer, the sailor and I. A one-shot shotgun had to be loaded each time. Surely he wouldn't try to shoot us all. All the same I checked for my escape route—but if I were to be the first target, as I said, I couldn't outrun a bullet. Inconvenient as it might have been, I decided Reginald was banking on setting up an accident. But it would have to be pretty convincing with all these witnesses. And his added incentive was to get Harriet gone before he had to give the prenup to Sophia.

Yet I couldn't get out of my mind how foolish he would be to try anything in public—drowning her in the bathtub would certainly be more efficacious.

The gun had somehow gotten into Reginald's hands while I was thinking.

"Pull!" he yelled, and the little clay pigeon that looked like an inverted, shallow bowl flew into the sky and Reginald shot. The clay bird shattered.

"Pull." Ditto. He shot five in a row. All hits. The

sailor and officer both expressed their awe.

"Man," I said bravely, "You sure can shoot."

"Thanks," he said, then turned to Harriet. "Wanna give it a try?" he asked, the gun hanging at his side.

"No, thank you," she said. "I wouldn't even be able to lift it."

"There's nothing to it," he said, lifting the gun to where he was a hair from hitting her with it. Maybe he could knock her overboard by accident? But he lowered the gun again, handed the officer five more dollars and hit five more clay pigeons in a row. No misses. My heart was pounding through the whole stellar performance, waiting for him to trip or something—maybe have an exaggerated reaction to the roll of the ship, lurch and pump a bullet into Harriet whereupon he would fall on the floor distraught, pounding the deck with his fists at his folly. I didn't doubt it would have been a good show. I didn't doubt he could have brought it off convincingly and hit her even if he wasn't looking her way. Any guy who could hit one of those little clay saucers at what must have been a hundred yards away, could hit an adult woman at eight feet without even trying.

But he didn't hit her. He didn't do anything but shoot the birds to perfection. It was all anticlimactic after that. We all sort of disappeared to our cabins and I tried to learn something from the experience. On the one hand, I thought it would be foolish of him to try to kill Harriet in front of witnesses. On the other hand, I thought he might *want* witnesses to verify that whatever happened certainly *was* accidental.

I went back to the earphones and prayed Harriet didn't take a bath before Sophia got the envelope. Of course, now I realized that he could easily sleight-of-hand the thing and not put the agreement in the envelope.

Another foolish notion swept through my mind. Perhaps I *was* imagining all this. Maybe Bluebeard *had* turned a new leaf. I would look like a fool, but I would be a fool with a hundred and fifty grand or more to salve the foolishness. In the meantime, perpetual vigilance would be the price of victory.

Hosanna! Harriet did not take a bath. I was cognizant of her sometime body odor, but tonight it would be a small price for me to pay. At the table, the mates had some bizarre conversations. Lillith Brown (Mrs. Chesty) brought up a subject on her mind, "A lady just married was on the ship for her honeymoon and her new husband dropped dead the first night out. She decided to go on with the cruise. She's on for the whole three months."

Reactions ranged from astonishment (Lillith), to, "I don't blame her" (Sophia). "She can do anything on the ship she could do at home—mourn, tear her hair out, or go on with her life. The thing is, on the ship she doesn't have to do the dishes."

"What would *you* do?" Sophia asked Lillith.

"I don't *know*. What would you *want* me to do, Chester?"

"Sure, go on, have fun. Everybody dies. No big deal."

"How about you, Harriet?" Lillith asked.

She twisted her taut lips. "I don't think I would want to go on."

"Why not?" Beefy asked.

"It just doesn't seem right. Not the seemly thing to do. Dancing on his grave, don't you see?"

"Reginald?" Sophia asked, "Should she?"

"That's her decision, but I feel fine, thanks."

"What would you do?" I asked Reginald.

"I'd be so broken up I'd be paralyzed. I'd have them put me off at the first opportunity. If I lost my Harriet I'd be a basketcase for sure."

"You're sweet," she said.

Sweet, maybe, but where's the envelope for Sophia, I thought.

Reginald read my mind. He pulled the envelope out of his pocket for all to see. "Sophia, would you be good enough to hold this for us until the cruise is over? It's some personal documents. You don't have to do anything, just put it in your safe. Would you be so kind?"

Sophia seemed baffled. She looked at the envelope as though it contained leprosy. "Well, sure, I guess so."

I breathed a sigh of relief. I thought we were home alive. Which only showed how little I knew.

21

The next day the ship made a failed attempt to land at Rarotonga in the Cook Islands, because the captain said the swells were too big for the landing craft to take us ashore. I said the captain was a sissy. But not to the captain.

At lunch Reginald brought up his height phobia again.

"Does any of you get the heebie-jeebies standing on deck with nothing between you and that precipitous drop to the cold and briny drink below? I'm always afraid the railing will give if I lean against it and I'll be a goner."

Sophia allowed as how she sometimes had those feelings.

Chesty Brown boomed, "That's ridiculous. Those railings are as strong as the Empire State Building. No one in history has fallen through one. If you have a death wish, you have to climb on top and jump over. It isn't going anywhere, that railing."

Everything Reginald said or did alerted me to some impending danger for Harriet. I was beginning to think it impossible for anyone to be in as much danger as I imagined for Harriet. Remember the boy and his pet wolf who kept crying "Boy, boy," or something. It didn't work out. Now every expression, every word, every thought set me thinking suspiciously, so that soon I was numbed to the dangers I imagined all around and wasn't sure I was in a position to separate the wheat from the whey. So after lunch, I lally-gagged around with Sophia so I could question her about the envelope.

Sophia and I tarried at the table. When we were alone, I said, "Sophia? Did you look in the envelope Reginald gave you?"

She gave me a perish-the-thinking look of dismay. "No—the instructions say not to look, just to hold it."

"Look," I said.

"Look?" She asked, puzzled. "Wouldn't that be a breach of confidence?"

"Maybe, but that's far less serious than what would result if we were wrong about what is in there."

"We? Wrong? I don't know what's in there."

"The prenuptial agreement, supposedly."

She made a sour face. "Is that any of our business?"

"It could be."

"What do you mean?"

"If Harriet's life is in danger."

"I don't follow you."

"You don't have to. Just let me look in the envelope."

"I don't know," she said thoughtfully. "When did you want to?"

"Now," I said.

"That soon?"

"Urgent."

She sighed. "Well, I guess if you want to come to my cabin we might talk some more...about it."

When we got inside the cabin, the door clicked automatically shut and locked behind us.

She quickly turned to face me and her arms wafted up to circle my neck. I was at once blown away at how little it took to dissuade me from my appointed course. Before I knew it, her mouth came onto mine and we were kissing with the passion of young lovers.

Her cabin was a lot smaller than my penthouse, and the queen-sized bed was not only the focal point, it took up most of the room. It was impossible to kiss like this in that tiny space devoted to floor without thinking bed.

But something told me I had to resist. The choice that flashed between my libidinous thought was I could self-ishly abandon my duty to my fiduciary, Harvey Cavendish, or I could pursue my appointed salvation of Harriet Himmelfarb—for my own selfish aims. It was as though the choice had come down to $150,000 or Sophia. I won't say paying for sex is unheard of, I just was not willing to pay $150,000 in this instance. I'm glad the stakes weren't lower, because the temptation would have obviously increased.

So, as Sophia pressured me toward the bed and I felt the side of the mattress press against the back of my calves, I struggled free. "Wait," I gasped for a passel of welcome air—

"Oh," Sophia said, disappointed.

"The envelope, please," I said.

"What is this?" she asked. "The Academy Awards?"

"You get the Oscar for the best seductress," I said, "and there's nothing I'd rather do than lie down with you."

"Except snoop in a private envelope," she said, slightly piqued.

"Someone's life is at stake," I said.

She gave a short laugh. "Now you get the Oscar for being the best overdramatic actor."

"Please…" I pleaded.

Sophia examined me as if she were at sea about my motives. I made my eyes as pleading as I could. "If I show it to you, can we snuggle?"

"Depends what's in it," I said, coyly.

"If what you expect is in it?"

She had me now, not by the vertically challenged hairs, but by *all* of them. "Okay," I said.

Finally she heaved a sigh of resigned regret and got up and pulled the letter from her top dresser drawer.

"Is that a very safe place for it?"

"Safe enough. There are no valuables in it."

"How do you know?"

"Well, you're right, I don't know. But I'm sure

Reginald would have said so, don't you think? And it feels just like a letter inside."

"A check?"

"Oh please. Why would he?"

With a little more coaxing and greasing her reluctance, she opened the envelope. She read the contents then handed it to me. "As advertised, I'd say," she said.

It was the agreement I wrote—the three-year one. Signed by Reginald and Harriet and dated. Legal.

"Would you let me take it to make a copy?"

She frowned. "Now that, I think, would be going too far. I have it. It is safe with me. I don't think Reginald feels too secure about this—makes him look like a weakling—so I'd better not go around his wishes any more than I already have."

Fair enough, I thought, and said as much. "But if you get near a copy machine, would *you* consider copying it?"

"I don't think so," she said. "I'll think about it, but I don't think so."

I thanked her and she said, "Now how about a little kiss? You have the sweetest blue eyes."

"I'd better not," I thought, but I'm so weak when it comes to the stronger sex.

And Lord was she good. I didn't regret a second of her horizontal challenge. Her enthusiasm was second to none. In fact she loved with such a vengeance, I wondered if there weren't some hidden psychological force that propelled her.

By the time I left her—with another long and longing kiss—I was exhausted. But I did have a sense of well being fostered in no small part by the erotic exercise, but also by seeing the prenuptial agreement safe in my lover's possession.

Somehow (I know not how) I made it up to my floating pad.

Back on the earphones, the subject was trying out the new camera. Harriet said she didn't feel like it just then, but Reginald seemed intent on a photo session on the deck. "I'm dying to get some pictures of you, babe. I've never seen you looking more ravishing. I think the marriage has taken ten years off your looks."

(Not your life, I hoped.)

"You're sweet, dear."

"So, I don't want to miss this honeymoon glow you have. I want to preserve it for posterity. Let's go down to the deck. The sun's just right."

"Oh, all right," she said. "You sure are persistent."

"Great, doll, I'm so excited about this. I want to get some of you and that vast ocean out there. Wear the blue dress will you? The one I like so much."

"Which blue dress?"

"The one that looks like the ocean."

There was a rustling sound, probably of the lady of the house swimming through her closet full of dresses. "This one?"

"That's the one. Put it on," he said, making kissing sounds again. "Oh, yeah, that's it. That's the one."

"Aren't you the incorrigible one," she said. "Skeet shooting, pictures, celebrating with toasts? I don't know if I can stand the pace."

"I'll give you a break after this. But we're getting to land tomorrow and I want to get you like you are walking on water. I've got an idea. You stand—I'll show you—and all we'll see is you and the ocean. You can take one of me first to get the idea of it."

"I don't know *how* to take pictures," was the protesting whine.

"I'll show you. All you do is press the button."

"That's all?"

"That's all."

The door closed and I opened mine. They went in the other direction and didn't pass my door. I didn't have a second to wait on this one. When I heard the elevator doors open and close, I ran to the steps and bounded down to floor eight—the promenade deck. I watched them make their way to the door and move outside. I followed and stood waiting to see what Reginald had in mind.

I found a hiding spot behind a part of the steel structure of the boat—a pillar? I don't know what you call it, but it was a bulky thing large enough to hide me. I think it had something to do with the lifeboats. The ship was pretty rocky, and I heard Harriet's voice say, "Couldn't we do this another day? I'm not too steady on my feet."

"It'll only take a minute," he said. They were standing at lifeboat station number ten, outside the windowless galley. The closest windows were to the dining rooms and could not be seen from this vantage point.

"Here's what I want you to do," he said, going over to the railing and opening a gate about three-feet wide and swinging it in. "Take a picture of me standing here with no gate to hold me, like I was walking on water." I peeked around and prayed for more foot traffic on the deck. There seemed to be virtually none. Then Sophia came by and I breathed a sigh of gratitude.

"Hi there," she said to Reginald. "What are you doing?"

"Just taking some pictures."

"May I watch?"

"Sure."

How foolish I felt. He certainly wasn't going to toss Harriet overboard with a witness. Unless he was so good at it that even the witness would be fooled and therefore be able to give testimony in his favor.

"Do you know how to work that camera, Sophia? Show Harriet will you? It's very simple. It's an automatic. Just press the button."

"Do you want me to take it?" our princess said.

"Yes!" Harriet said. "Then I can go in, this is too rocky to be out." She made a motion of unsteadiness with her swaying body.

"No, I want to take you here. I'm just showing you what to do. It'll only be a second."

So I thought with Sophia out there, I could appear. I

did so while Reginald was striking a ridiculous pose with his arms floating in air, out to his side in one of those ta-dah poses.

"Now you try it," he said. "Oh, Gil. What are you doing here?" I noticed his attitude seemed to change from how he greeted Sophia. Maybe I imagined it, but Sophia seemed unusually cool toward me herself.

"Just out for some air."

"Oh," he said. "Well, we're taking some pictures."

"I see that."

"Could you give us some room here?"

"Will I be in the picture standing here?"

"No, but I feel a little crowded. This is a mood piece and I'm afraid you'll spoil it."

"I promise not to," I said. "I'd like to see what you're doing."

"Gil," Sophia said, "let's walk around the deck." I stood beside where she was taking Reginald's picture and she turned to me to whisper, "He seems a little funny. I think we should leave them alone."

"That's why I don't want to," I whispered back. Maybe that ship-engine sound kept him from hearing, but I'm not sure. Reginald came back to us with an angry frown on his face.

"Okay, Harriet, your turn," he said.

"What do you want me to do?" she asked insouciantly.

"Same as I did."

"On the edge like that? With no railing? I don't think I want to do that," she said. "It doesn't look safe."

"It's perfectly safe. Hold onto the railing if you must."

"Are you crazy?" I said. "The way this boat is rocking, this is insanity. Don't you do it, Harriet."

"Oh, Gil," Sophia said. "It's a harmless picture. You're overreacting."

"Maybe, but I'd like to keep her alive. This trick shot can be done a million safer ways."

146

"Look pal," Reginald turned on me in anger. "Just butt out, will you! You are getting very tiresome the way you push yourself into all our affairs. Now this is a *private* thing so why don't you buzz off?"

"I'm not buzzing off because I see a lot of danger here. Maybe you don't see it," I said looking through him like an x-ray trying to see the sinister bones in his body, "and maybe—you do."

Then Reginald grabbed Harriet by the wrist and pulled her toward the edge. They tripped once en route, and I grabbed her other outstretched wrist. She was yelping in terror and I couldn't blame her. Suddenly Sophia got agitated. "Oh, Gil, let them alone."

"So he can throw her overboard?"

"Oh, he's not going to do any such thing."

"No? Look at him."

Sophia astonishingly put her arms around my waist and started to pull me away from Harriet. Disturbing news, this. Fortunately she was no pillar of strength, but she was enough distraction to throw me off balance, and I nearly lost my hold of Harriet, who was now a believer and crying in agony.

"My God, Sophia," I said. "You're in on this." I felt a stab of pain in my heart. I thought it was love, and I'd only been used. What a stupid fool I had been.

On the edge of the deck with nothing between us and a very wet coffin, Reginald stood pulling Harriet. This certainly was no subtle accident. This was murder, pure and simple, and it was we two against those two and these odds were far from even. Reginald was a lot stronger than I was, and anybody was stronger than Harriet.

I looked at Reginald. He needed a shave, and that six o'clock shadow was *blue!*

The deck was slick which may have helped the underdogs. I shook Sophia off with some effort, sending her sprawling stunned across the deck. Then I grabbed Harriet by the waist for more leverage. I propped my foot against an upright on the stationary railing and pulled. Reginald pulled the other way. In our tussle, he maneuvered himself into position opposite the opening so he was protected too. His face had that tormented Bluebeard look. Looking at that wretched countenance, so different than Reginald's happy face, was enough to make me want to jump.

The great swells of the ocean were rocking the ship like a toy. Sea spray was hitting us making the deck super slick.

Reginald was holding the railing on one side of the opening, I was on the other. Only Harriet was exposed now. We pulled her back and forth. She never let up her scream—but no one came. Her feet were slipping and sliding on the sloppy deck. She looked like a rag doll between two selfish little boys. Though it seemed like an eternity, it was only a matter of seconds. Reginald slipped and I was able to pull Harriet to the protection of my railing where I kicked out at Reginald, startling him. Then I gave him what I thought was a karate chop to his arm, and he let out a yelp and loosened his grip long enough to permit one kick to his stomach which sent him flying, screaming into the water. He disappeared without a trace.

My heart was pounding, my throat was dry. I was gasping for breath when Sophia shouted, "Gil! You murdered him!"

"Just in time, too," I gulped more air. I was astonished *I* was still alive and the athletic Bluebeard was safe in the drink. "He was about to murder Harriet."

"He was not! He was the kindest, gentlest, most generous man I ever knew." And she broke into uncontrollable sobs.

22

Sophia ran screaming somewhere, and in time they stopped the ship. Three lifeboats were lowered and the search began for Reginald Windsor a.k.a. Fred Kantor, a.k.a. Bluebeard. It appeared to me they used due diligence, the boats made circles, widening from different centers at three points closest to where they calculated Reginald had gone overboard. I was surprised at just how far away they were from where the ship was floating dead, as they say, in the water. It looked to me like at least a half-mile.

I admit to mixed feelings about the search. If they did find him and revive him and return him to the ship, it wouldn't surprise me to hear him talk his way out of it with some fantastic story, similar, no doubt, to the aftermath of some of his earlier wives' deaths. So while I couldn't really bring myself to wish anyone dead, I was likewise unable to pull for Reginald's rescue.

Seamen have an understanding of these matters and they searched as long as they could hold out any hope. They spoke of the possibility of a broken neck or back from the fall, the temperature of the water, sharks—all of which seemed just desserts for Bluebeard. But I was never at ease. Not even when the sailors came back empty-handed and the rescue boats were hoisted back in place, not when the ship got underway again.

A hasty investigation was made by the officer the

captain designated for such duty. He had a beard like the ship's doctor and was a pretty serious dish of fish. But he was thoughtful and, I'd have to say, competent. He talked to the three surviving eyewitnesses and it resulted, alas, in Sophia's relegation to the clink.

After dinner, I went to see Sophia in the ship's slammer. It was a space not likely to be pictured in the ship's brochure when they talk about the life of a sybarite. Though there was a chair in her cell, she preferred to sit on the bed, slumped against the back wall in a posture of insouciance. Her eyes were red from marathon crying. I took the chair, deciding it was less threatening than standing.

She looked up at me as though I had just killed her best friend, which, in a way, I had.

"I'm sorry, Sophia," I said, setting aside my personal disappointment, not to say anger.

She only glared at me.

"I don't get it, Sophia," I said. "Did you know Reginald *before* we sailed?"

She glared, but I saw that red-eyed face dip barely perceptively. "He was the most wonderful man I have ever known," she said without moving a muscle. "And *you* killed him."

"To keep him from killing Harriet," I argued.

She shook her head. "He only wanted to take her picture."

Yeah, I thought, on the bottom of the ocean—but now the cameraman was there instead. That would be her defense. She was only assisting in a photography session.

"I suppose in your predicament I won't carp about what we had between us. You were trying to distract me—and you were awfully good at it, I must say."

"You killed him, and I'm the one in jail." She ignored me—as though we never happened, then shook her head and let out a miserable groan. "He was my tennis coach," she explained, talking now to assuage her loneliness. "I loved him and he loved me as no other man had ever…"

150

I nodded. It was a familiar story by now. He sure knew how to make a woman feel good. "His past didn't scare you?"

Her little whimper might have passed for a laugh in happier circumstances.

"I still don't get it, Sophia," I said. "How did you happen to come aboard? Did you talk it over with Reginald? Did he want you to?"

"He didn't want to be apart from me," she said. "He was the third husband I told you about—only we weren't married. He got me off gambling," she shook her head. "The only one who could. Such a wonderful man. He was my savior."

"So he paid for your trip?"

She nodded.

"But where did he get the money? He's not—was not—wealthy, was he?"

"Oh," she waved a tired hand at me. It was obvious the entire experience had sucked the life out of her. "He'd gotten some from his ninth. But Harriet..." she trailed off—

"Was going to be his big score," I supplied.

She didn't protest. She dropped her eyelids instead. It was all she could muster.

"But...Harriet...?"

"She was just a convenient meal ticket," she said. "He really loved me."

I nodded, more in amazement than agreement. Reginald Windsor was some man. Like a bee making the rounds, pollinating infertile flowers, making them feel good. Taking money from one to amuse another. But always moving on as if he were a good Samaritan whose touch could rejuvenate the rejected.

"Oh—just one more thing, Sophia—where did you learn about palms?"

"My second husband—he was a palm nut from Florida." She shrugged. "Just rubbed off on me, I guess. Oh, by the way, thanks for going with me to the botanic garden. I enjoyed it."

I had too, but I couldn't say so now. Instead it jogged my memory—back to that day.

"And *you* threw that rock down on me in Tahiti? After what passed between us in the botanic garden?"

"I did it for Reginald," she said like a zombie. "I would do...have done *any*thing for Reginald."

"How did you even lift it?"

"It wasn't very heavy. Volcanic," she explained. "Sharp edges."

I grunted. Try as I might, I couldn't reconcile our sport in the botanic garden with the sport of hurling razor sharp volcanic rock at your lover. Perhaps I'm old fashioned.

I gave Sophia a magnanimous kiss on her forehead, a pat on the shoulder and a hug I hoped was reassuring. But I had to admit to myself, I was glad she was in and I was out. It could easily have been the other way around. I left her sad and red-eyed, to her memories.

Back in my cabin, I pulled the recording set out of commission, then took on the self-appointed task of commiserating with Harriet in her grief. You wouldn't think she would be feeling anything but relief and gratitude at that juncture, but she was feeling grief, and I thought under the circumstances I should help her through it.

It took a long time and a herculean effort for Harriet to answer the door. She appeared in the white terry cloth robe provided by the cruise line for the penthouse customers. "Yes?" she said, as though I were a brush salesman disturbing the sanctity of her home. It was more with reluctance than graciousness that she allowed me into her cabin where we sat on perpendicular couches, I with my hands away from my body, caressing the leather, she with her hands folded in her lap.

I was surprised that she was not entirely comfortable with me or grateful for my concern. She somehow managed to see me as the person who caused her husband's death, rather than the person who saved her life.

I didn't try too hard to disabuse her of that notion.

Rather, I sat patiently with her and listened to her self-absorbed agony.

"What was that other woman doing there?"

"Sophia? That other woman was in cahoots with Reginald. I didn't realize it until she started telling us what a wonderful guy he was—after she told me she couldn't stand him and what not. And to think she was holding the prenuptial agreement. She just turned to jelly after he fell. Can you imagine what would have happened to that agreement if *you* had gone overboard? They've got her locked up as an accomplice to an attempted murder. They tell me she claims not to want to live without her beloved Reginald."

"How could he want to have anything to do with her when he had *me?*" Harriet wanted to know. "And I thought she was after *you!*"

"Some ruse, I guess," trying to be indifferent. "And Reginald—was just Reginald. Women were trophies. Once he got one, he went on to the next. He couldn't help himself."

"He said he *loved* me," Harriet sniffled, harried.

"And I believe he did. He just loved a lot of women at the same time—was constitutionally unable to limit himself to one. He admitted it. Except he just started maintaining that he was too old."

"Yes—he told me that often, don't you know?"

I nodded to her rhetorical question. "He was so convincing," I said, "I think he actually convinced himself."

"I still love him, you know," she said. "I only wish you hadn't pushed him off the ship. Was that really necessary?"

"I didn't push him, really. He was a much stronger man than I. In any contest of strength, he would have won, palms down. But he had pulled you to the edge and that put *him* on the edge. I was pulling you away from the water, he was pulling toward it. I hit his arm to get him to release you, and he must have been so surprised that a wimp like me could hit him with so much force that he slipped and fell overboard." All right, I omitted a few brutal details. Why make her feel worse about me?

"But couldn't you have gone in after him?"

I smiled at her. "Not me," I said. "I'm surprised Sophia didn't go after him."

"I'm so sad," she said. "He loved me," she lamented with such a poignant sense of loss that I felt sorry for her. But I understood what she meant and what she wanted me to understand—at seventy-six, she had found a man to pay her some attention, and that was no mean feat. I had come between them, and even though I may have saved her life in the process I had cost her an admirer, and, at her age, admirers were not that easy to come by, legitimate or not.

She said she couldn't face the Browns at the table and would prefer to have dinner in her room, which she did. I stayed with her that night for dinner and I think she was grateful, though I also thought she felt it her due.

I went to the table for breakfast. We had docked in Aukland and Chesty and Lillith were already assaulting a stack of pancakes and a piece of dry toast, respectively.

"There he is!" Chesty boomed, his fork full of pancakes suspended in midair. "What gives? Where's the grand *dame?* Lot of messy goings on. They tell us that looker Sophia was involved. Must've been quite an actress. I'd a never guessed she and that phony Reginald were a team."

"Me neither," I said. "We're getting off here," I said. "I'm accompanying Harriet home. It's a little early, but I think she needs some help. Sophia is going to be detained until they can determine where to try her. I think they better put a suicide watch on her, because of the two women, she was the harder hit."

Sophia would later be released by a district attorney who realized she was just a hapless woman who might have caused some harm to an innocent woman, but didn't—a lonely woman who was given a small window of self esteem by a charlatan and who was coincidentally present at his death.

In Aukland, New Zealand, I called Harvey with the news and he seemed pleased. He said he would meet us at the airport in Los Angeles and take his mother to his home while she recuperated.

On the Air New Zealand flight from Aukland to Los Angeles, Harriet said she was ready to write a will. She still wasn't sure how she would make her bequests, but was thinking of some charities to give a good chunk to.

Back home Harriet pulled herself out of her funk and began "dating" again. It is a mystery to me where the men come from, but one shouldn't underestimate the drawing power of a million-a-year income, tax-free.

I got home and found my palms and cycads thriving. I had some new growth on a couple of rare *Encephalartos*— my *munchii* and my *dolomiticus.*

Tyranny Rex was blowing away on some glass goblets she was lately trying her lungs at.

"Oh, dear," she said, "you're back already. I'm afraid I haven't prepared any dinner."

"Funny thing," I said. "I'm not that hungry."

Excerpts from *The Unlucky Seven*
A Gil Yates Private Investigator Novel
By Alistair Boyle

"How'd the audition go?" I asked as he hustled into the narrow deli with his duffel bag slung on a shoulder. In that section of the Big Applesauce, storefronts rented by the front-foot. So you had a lot of places that were about eight-feet wide and three-miles deep. The best tables were those you could reach without falling over from heat exhaustion.

"I was pleased," he said. "Trouble is, *they* have to be pleased, so you're always on pins and needles."

We made our way to a table, a distance of what some years ago would have constituted a summer vacation.

When we sat, he put his duffel bag on the floor at his feet, and said, "I ran into Greg at the audition—I asked him to join us when he finished—I hope that's all right. I haven't seen him in ages."

I waved a hand, as though I was one blasé dude. Actually, I was a little disappointed that my son wanted a buddy along for our too-infrequent meetings.

"Oh, here's Greg"—and he seemed to light up more at the sight of Greg than he had for his own father.

Greg slid into the chair next to August. They smiled, touched, rolled their eyes and raised their eyebrows, as they relived the audition and catted about some of their competition.

The waitress dragged herself to the table, as though under some internal protest. She took out her pad and wet her finger, then applied it to flip to the appropriate page.

That was, she made clear, the sum total of the communicative effort she was willing to expend in our behalf. I ordered the pastrami with everything; August and Greg agreed to split one of those concoctions recommended by Anorexics Anonymous.

I tried to bring Greg into the conversation. Though what I was doing, was trying to bring myself into the conversation.

"What do you guys think of this conspiracy bomber?"

"The Seven guy?" Greg said. "Creepy." I'm not sure August knew who we were talking about. He never seemed too taken with murder and mayhem. "Who were the victims?—Fenster of Softex, of course. The CIA guy, and who was the other one?"

"Philip Carlisle—United Motors."

Greg shrugged, "Big, rich, powerful guys. Maybe that's a risk you have to take."

"You think so?" I said. "Random killings?"

"Aren't random," Greg said. "Anything but. Very individual—targeted."

"You think there could be something to the idea seven people ruled the world?"

"I've heard crazier stuff," Greg said.

"You?" I asked August.

"I won't go for any number of world rulers unless fearless Elbert August Wemple is among them."

I'll say this for the kid, he knew how to win my approval.

"Made a lot of enemies," Greg mumbled.

"What's that?"

"Some of those guys made a lot of enemies. Take Fenster. Stepped on a lot of bodies to get where he is. There's a guy *I* could believe ruled the world."

"Why?"

"Nobody gets in his way. And the competition along the way didn't roll over and play dead. He had to roll them over. A young kid like that isn't going to be worth eight to ten billion without ruffling a few feathers."

"Yeah, I guess."

"But it's a real tragedy. He just got married—built a huge house."

"But you aren't surprised somebody killed him?"

"No. When you are so successful and so beloved in some quarters, you are bound to engender the opposite feelings in equal magnitude."

"Do you know anything about the other victims of

this latest bomber?"

"Nah. Just Fenster."

"Nothing that would tie them up?"

"No, except that it is virtually impossible to live in the world and *not* be tied up with Bob Fenster. If having ties to him and his product was the criterion for killing, you'd have to nuke the whole country."

We finished our sandwiches, and I left Miss Congeniality a tip commensurate with her charm and grace.

I thanked Greg for his information, and asked if I might call him if I had more questions.

"I'll keep in touch with August," he said. "I move around a lot."

My son and I hugged briefly, and I thought I put a little more into it than he did.

August and Greg disappeared down the street. They seemed quite content to have put me behind them. The only thing that salved my feelings was August had not asked about his mother.

Excerpts from *The Missing Link*
A Gil Yates Private Investigator Novel
By Alistair Boyle

He certainly was fond of talking. More than I am
fond of listening. And of all places to experience logorrhea, a
meeting of palm nuts should rightfully be near the bottom.
There is zero communication with palm trees. Oh, a lot of
people talk to them, but there is no documentary proof that
any of them have ever talked back.

My new buddy is a gardener for one of the super-rich.
Mr. Rich's got a whale of a palm collection, so Jack Kimback
is here to bone up.

Now Jack gets to the meat of the thing. His boss,
who is just too famous, in an illicit sort of way, to mention, is
looking for a private detective to find his daughter.

He has interviewed every known agency, tried a few,
and doesn't like any of them. He is apparently a very picky
man, as can be seen in his hiring this erudite, well-spoken
young man to tend his palms.

Said Megabucks has also had it with the cops and the
missing persons folks. A man that rich, his gardener says, is
used to buying what he wants, but his money, this time, isn't
cutting the ketchup.

If you have ever felt possessed by the devil, you know
how I felt when I heard the following words come out of my
mouth:

"Oh, I just happen to *be* a private detective."

Jack's eyebrows hit the ceiling. You could tell he was
skeptical that a mealy-mouthed guy like me would be in such
a macho line of work.

It seemed like a harmless tease at first. I didn't look
on it as a lie, exactly. A lark. I thought it would go no further. Any time now, I would set him straight–tell him I was
only joking. But the more he told me, the more intrigued I
became, and the less impetus I had for telling the technical
truth.

You know what the "technical truth" is. It is something that only serves the science of mathematics. Every other human endeavor is necessarily fraught with nuances, with shadings, with spared feelings, with personal aggrandizement. Call a spade a spade? Only when you are playing cards.

"I'll give him your card," Jack said, putting his hand out for a card, as though that would be an easy end to it.

"I don't have cards," I heard myself say, "that's for small-timers."

His eyebrows were on the rise again.

"Well, give me your name and office address, he'll have somebody check you out."

"I'm not a guy who sits in an office," I said, astonishing even myself with the dire depths of my deception. "Results is my middle name. And," I added with just the right touch of hauteur, "my phone is unlisted."

"So how do people get a hold of you?"

"They don't," I said. "I call them."

Now the dark eyebrows went whacko. "You don't know my boss," he said.

"And maybe I'd be just as well-off getting through life without knowing him."

He frowned and gave a curt nod that he must have thought was noncommittal.

"Tell you what," I said. "Let him know we talked. I'll call you in a couple days. If he's interested, I'll meet him." Then I added, unknowingly, the clincher: "By the way, I work like the ambulance-chasing lawyers: I don't find his daughter, I don't get paid."

A smile crossed his face, like a man realizing the razor being held at his neck was just for shaving. "He'll like that," he said, writing his phone number on a photocopy of a walking tour of the palms at Bernuli Junior College. "Sometimes he's so tight, he squeaks."

"She was anorexic," he said softly, a little ashamed. "Bulimic. I tried to help her. I couldn't do anything. I put her in an institution. The best money could buy," he hastened to add, unnecessarily. He paused to control his breathing–to drain the flush from his face. "She escaped. Hasn't been seen since."

"How long ago?"

"Nine months or so."

"Been to the police? The FBI? Missing persons?"

He stared at me as though it were a naive question. "She's an adult. They seemed to spit on me. They went through some motions," he said. "Nothing came of it." Then he added, as though it surprised him, "I think they resented me."

"Why?"

"The way they acted. What do cops make now–twenty, thirty a year? Bound to be some resentment," he said, waving his hand to encompass his expensive property. "I never felt comfortable with them."

"Do you feel comfortable with me?"

He gave me the frozen fish eye. "I don't know yet."

"What is it you want? Just a notice that she is alive–or dead–or physical possession?"

He looked at me as though his nose were a gunsight. "Well, I would expect to see her," he said. "I mean, I don't doubt your integrity, but I'd have to have the physical evidence."

"Is it possible she won't want to see you?"

Darts came through the eyes. "Why would she not?" he faltered. I think I heard his voice break. "Of course...it's...possible." He put a spin on "possible," like anything was possible but he would just as soon not think it could be in this case. When he regained his composure, he asked, "So what would you charge?"

Here we were at the moment of truth. I had rehearsed my blasé response to this inevitable question in front of the bathroom mirror in our tract house. I had honed it to as near believable perfection as I was capable of bringing off. But now my tongue seemed to stick to my lower teeth. Michael Hadaad didn't let his gaze waver. Finally I shook my head, once. "Phew," I said with as much bravado as my thumping heart would allow. "Gonna be expensive."

"How expensive?" he asked, cocking an eye of suspicion.

"Not so simple," I said. "I bring her here and she's happy to come, I'd settle for two hundred."

"Two hundred dollars?" He thought he had gotten lucky.

"Two hundred thousand," I corrected him.

"Two..." he choked. "That's ridiculous!"

This is where my art came in. I nodded, the soul of understanding, and stood to leave. I nodded again, in acknowledgment of his hospitality, and said, "I quite understand. My fees are a lot higher than the run of the mill. There are many available for a lot less."

He just stared at me, as though I were the first person to ever walk out on him. For my part, I was not as bummed at the prospect of losing the case or the fee–it was a lark anyway–as I was of losing the opportunity to see his palm collection.

I turned to leave. I had not taken three steps when I heard the mighty Michael Hadaad say, "No, wait."

I smiled to myself before I turned. Now I cocked my eye–as he had done so expertly.

He answered: "You had the guts to get up. Most people can't see past their fee. Sit down."

I did.

"Is there room for negotiation?"

"I don't nickel and dime," I said. "I don't submit chits for meals and gas. But I'm afraid I've only given you the low side."

Up went the eyelids.

I nodded. God, I thought, is he buying this? But how could he? "If she doesn't want to come, it will be a half-million."

He sank back in his chair. I stood again, but faced him. "I quite understand your reluctance, Mr. Hadaad. I am used to working for the extremely wealthy, exclusively."

He waved me back into my seat, without looking.

Excerpts from *The Con*
A Gil Yates Private Investigator Novel
By Alistair Boyle

I have always had a soft spot in my heart for a con man. I'm not sure why. He is usually a man (sorry, ladies, most of them seem to be men) who makes his living out-smarting those who are smarter than he is.

He usually plays on the greed and the get-rich-without-working nature of people who have had more education and advantages than he had. People who should know better.

So looking for the most successful and most elusive con man was an assignment I couldn't resist.

The call came from the big man himself, Franklin d'Lacy. There was no baloney with an intermediary secretary. No executive wait while the honcho cleared his throat.

"Mr. Yates," he spoke clearly, distinctly into my voice mail at the phone company, with a clipped diction that put you in mind of the British Empire. It was only an affectation, though a very good one. "Your services have been recommended to me by a member of our board, and I would appreciate a return phone call at your earliest convenience."

d'Lacy was all smiles as he rose to greet me. "So good of you to come, Yates," he beamed. I could see in a flash why he was so good at raising bucks for his museum. (He always referred to it as "my museum". It didn't win him any extra friends.)

He was the quintessential salesman, but way too suave for used cars. High-end real estate, maybe, or main-frame computers.

He struck me as a guy sensitive of his height, but he wasn't that short. At five foot, eleven-some inches I was taller, but only by a couple of inches. He was dressed in one of those banker, pin-stripe, Brooks Brothers worsteds.

He was tan, had enough hair for the whole board of

directors and was fit as a cello. Did some jogging in the early morning to get the juices flowing, and after work a couple nights a week worked out those juices on a personal trainer of whom, it was said, he had carnal knowledge.

"Hold the calls, Miss Craig," he said, as the young woman backed out of the room. Do you suppose she sensed my predilection to stare at her sculptured buns? Everything here was a work of art—so much to stare at. The staff, I decided, was selected for their stare appeal, just like Hammurabi's nickels and dimes and Titian's oils.

So you could tell pin-stripe d'Lacy from your run-of-the-mill banker, he wore a gardenia in his jacket buttonhole. I could smell it from where I sat across his Brazilian rosewood desk, which was the genuine article, not the laminate, and was, roughly, the size of Brazil.

I couldn't get over how darn gracious he was. "Are you comfortable in that chair? May I get you something to drink?"

"Thanks, I'm fine."

"Well," he said, taking his measure of me down a nose that could have held its own with the marble statues in the foyer, "Michael Hadaad speaks very highly of you."

I almost fell off my chair. Michael Hadaad? The same guy who tried to clean out my sinuses with a bullet rather than turn over my fee after I had accomplished his goal? He was the last guy in the world I would expect to recommend me.

Michael Hadaad is my pseudonym for this slightly tarnished megabucks who put me through loops on my first case, from which I was grateful to escape with my skin.

d'Lacy seemed amused at my reaction. He was looking at me over the little temple he had made with his manicured fingertips. I could tell he wanted in the worst way to be British. It represented class to him.

"Michael is on our board, you know," he said.

"No, I..."

"Given us a nice piece of change over the years, I daresay."

I nodded. Why else would that creep be on

LAMMA's board of directors?

"Of course, he said you were a rank amateur. 'Childish,' was, I believe, the way he put it. 'A wimp, impossible to reason with'..."

"So why...?"

"Why is obvious, isn't it? You solved his problem. Look here, Yates, I'm a results-oriented guy. I wouldn't have made my museum a world-class institution if I hadn't been. Why, I'd work with a wooden-legged centipede if he brought me the pigeon."

Was there, I wondered, buried in there, flattery?

"He also told me the most remarkable thing about you," he said.

"Oh?"

Franklin d'Lacy nodded. "Said you worked exclusively on a contingency basis." He was especially amused when he said, "Michael quoted you as saying a thousand a day and expenses was tacky."

"Well, perhaps I..."

"That's what interests me," d'Lacy said. "That, and the fact that Michael assures me you are an absolute nut for privacy and secrecy. Discretion, he says, is your byword. No business cards, no office, not even," this he pronounced with relish, "a license."

Was Franklin d'Lacy really winking at me?

"Of course, I understand a contingency fee comes a lot higher than I could buy one of those small-timers, but if you achieve my goal, I will pay you one million dollars."

Also Available from Allen A. Knoll, Publishers
Books for Intelligent People Who Read for Fun

The Unlucky Seven: A Gil Yates Private Investigator Novel
By Alistair Boyle
Do seven people rule the world? Someone thinks so and is systematically sending bombs to kill each of these seven wealthy and influential men. Three are dead already by the time Yates arrives on the scene. $20

The Con: A Gil Yates Private Investigator Novel
By Alistair Boyle
Gil Yates backs into the high-stakes art forgery world, bringing the danger, romance and humor that Boyle's fans love. $19.95

The Missing Link: A Gil Yates Private Investigator novel
By Alistair Boyle
A desperate and ruthless father demands that Gil bring him his missing daughter. The game quickly turns deadly with each unburied secret, until Gil's own life hangs by a thread. $19.95

The Snatch
By David Champion
Two cops whose methods are polar opposites—in love with the same kidnapped woman—race against time and each other to save her. From Los Angeles' lowlands to its highest mountain, *The Snatch* races at breakneck speed to a crashing climax. $19.95

Celebrity Trouble: A Bomber Hanson Mystery
By David Champion
Unspeakable accusations of child molestation against mega star Steven Shag prompt him to call Bomber Hanson. Courtroom theatrics abound as the nature of man unfolds in this latest of the acclaimed Bomber Hanson series. $20

166

The Mountain Massacres: A Bomber Hanson Mystery
By David Champion
In this riveting, edge-of-your-seat suspense drama, world-famous attorney Bomber Hanson and his engaging son Tod explore perplexing and mysterious deaths in a remote mountain community. $14.95

Nobody Roots for Goliath: A Bomber Hanson Mystery
By David Champion
Larger-than-life Attorney Bomber Hanson and his son Tod take on the big guns—the tobacco industry. Is it responsible for killing their client? $22.95

Flip Side: A Novel of Suspense:
By Theodore Roosevelt Gardner II
Can a murder trial really have two such conflicting perspectives? A novel unique in content and format, *Flip Side* gives us two heart stopping versions of the same high-profile multiple-murder case. $22

Order from your bookstore, library, or from Allen A. Knoll, Publishers at (800) 777-7623. Or send a check for the amount of the book, plus $3.00 shipping and handling for the first book, $1.50 for each additional book, (plus 7 ¼% tax for California residents) to:

Allen A. Knoll, Publishers
200 West Victoria Street
Santa Barbara, Ca 93101

Credit cards also accepted.
Please call if you have any questions (800) 777-7623, or if you would like to receive a free Knoll Publishers catalog.